KARRIE'S THORN

a novel

KARRIE'S THORN

a novel

One Girl's *Faith* Journey

REV. CHERYL ANNE KINCAID

AMBASSADOR INTERNATIONAL

GREENVILLE, SOUTH CAROLINA & BELFAST, NORTHERN IRELAND

www.ambassador-international.com

Karrie's Thorn: A Novel

ISBN: 978-1-62020-751-2
eISBN: 978-1-62020-671-3

Cover Design by Hannah Linder Designs
Interior Typesetting by Hannah Nichols
eBook Conversion by Anna Riebe Raats

Scripture quotations are taken from the Holy Bible, New Living Translation, copyright ©1996, 2004, 2015 by Tyndale House Foundation. Used by permission of Tyndale House Publishers, Carol Stream, Illinois 60188. All rights reserved.

This is a work of fiction. Names, characters, and incidents are all products of the author's imagination or are used for fictional purposes. Any resemblance to actual events or persons, living or dead, is entirely coincidental. Any mentioned brand names, places, and trademarks remain the property of their respective owners, bear no association with the author or the publisher, and are used for fictional purposes only.

AMBASSADOR INTERNATIONAL
Emerald House
411 University Ridge, Suite B14
Greenville, SC 29601, USA
www.ambassador-international.com

AMBASSADOR BOOKS
The Mount
2 Woodstock Link
Belfast, BT6 8DD, Northern Ireland, UK
www.ambassadormedia.co.uk

The colophon is a trademark of Ambassador, a Christian publishing company.

To all the women and men, who suffer in silence, I pray this book helps you find your voice.

Chapter 1

A splinter had slipped beneath the surface of Karrie's arm. A dark brown slender thorn protruded from a thin layer of her freckled skin. It was surrounded by a pink halo, and Karrie thought it was beautiful.

"Do you want me to take that out?" Grandma said while wiping the dirt off her hands onto her old apron dress. She bent down to examine Karrie's hand.

Light, warm winds blew through the canyon where they had been gardening, which dried her grandma's sweat into brown lines that ran across her winkled forehead. Karrie stood on her tiptoes looking over Grandma's shoulder so she could see the garden. It sloped down the side of a California canyon like a patchwork quilt that had been causally thrown over the side of a bed. The wind carried the smells of onions, dried corn, sunflowers, and, of course, Grandma. Karrie loved the smell of Grandma's garden, and Grandma.

Grandma's house and garden were in a part of the town that Karrie imagined had been misplaced during a late-night meeting in the mayor's office. It seemed as though the larger, more fashionable part of the city didn't bother looking for it because they knew they could do just as well without it.

From Grandma's porch, she could see the tall buildings of the downtown shopping mall. But the sleek, perfectly paved streets and the fashionable coffee shops, full of beautiful people were nowhere to be found near Karrie's or Grandma's house. The downtown mall was only five miles away, but the white wooden house on the edge of the canyon and under the shadow of a freeway was a different world from where those downtown buildings stood.

At the mall, people walked freely, chattering and laughing while lingering in and out of chic dress shops and restaurants. Men and women in tailored business suits ran from one building to another, only occasionally looking up from their smart phones.

On the streets near Karrie's house, people fearfully walked with their heads down, careful not to catch the eye of anyone passing by. They hid their purses under their coats while suspiciously looking over their shoulders as they rushed from one bus to another. They quickened their pace as they ran home when the sky cooled with the first breath of dusk. Middle school–aged kids with hard, angry faces gathered on the street corners. Every three blocks were dressed with liquor stores. These stores were guarded by three or four men with weary eyes. While waiting for a bus, Karrie had often stared at their long faces weighed down with disappointment as their tired eyes gazed at the buses and cars that just passed them by without notice.

Grandma's house was sectioned off from the rest of the neighborhood by a long, sloping driveway that led into the canyon. Deeper in the canyon, on the side of Grandma's garden there was, hidden in an overgrown rose-bush, a rusted old Victorian bench swing. Karrie was sure that some day a re-porter from News Channel 10 would discover that the old bench swing was owned by a great, elegant lady from London who was British royalty. That day, the reporter would come out to Grandma's house with television cam-eras to tell the whole world about the long-lost swing and the famous lady who owned it; then the world would discover Grandma's garden. Grandma and Karrie's family would become famous and rich. Grandma would buy a long silk dress with golden roses embroidered along the collar and high-heeled shoes, and Karrie could eat all the ice cream cones she wanted from the thrifty drugstore.

Grandma ran her finger gently over the thorn in Karrie's thumb, and the red halo bump smoothed out under Grandma's touch. It turned white, and then it bounced back again, rosy pink. Grandma wrinkled her face. "Karrie, I think that has to come out."

"No," said Karrie, "don't take it out yet. I want to show it to Pastor Will."

Last Sunday, Pastor Will had talked about the scars on Jesus's hands and said His scars showed the glory of God. Then he'd said, "Now just because you trust God, don't go thinking you won't have any scars. Indeed, some of the godliest people in our congregation have the greatest scars. You might say they have, as the apostle Paul had, thorns in the flesh."

Then Pastor Will had started to talk about people with these "thorns." At that moment, Karrie wished she had a thorn she could show Pastor Will that would testify to her love for Jesus. But Karrie had never had a thorn or splinter stuck in her skin—until now. She would show it to Pastor Will, and she knew he would admire it.

Grandma turned her head to one side and looked at Karrie as if she was trying to figure something out.

"I gotta get home to get ready for youth club at the church," said Karrie. "Bye, Grandma." She kissed Grandma and then began to climb up the long, sloping drive to the busy street.

Once someone walked up Grandma's driveway into the busy street that ran above her house, they entered a harder world. That hard street could never imagine there was a little farmhouse at the foot of a long, sloping driveway and that the farmhouse possessed a lovely garden of Karrie's grandma's making.

But Karrie did not see the hard streets today. Her thoughts were about what the pastor would say when he saw her thorn. *Yes. I'll show my thumb to Pastor Will, and he will say, "Karrie, that is exactly what I was talking about!"* The next Sunday, he would ask Karrie to come to the front of the church to show all the grown-ups her thorn, and they would look at her hand and smile and say, "Yes, yes, just like the preacher was saying. Just like he was saying!"

When Karrie reached her house, she pushed open the front door and heard the clink of empty wine bottles rolling across the floor. Her father was lying across a pile of unfolded laundry strewn across the couch. Soured wine on her father's breath was the worst smell in the world. *I wish I could smell Grandma's garden in this place.* Karrie maneuvered her way to the bathroom over the weekly debris of old newspaper and trash that constantly cluttered the living room.

Inside the bathroom, she turned on the cold water and let it run over her hands, peeling away the brown veneer of soil from the garden. Then she ran into her room to find her favorite white tank top and a pair of her favorite blue jeans. She had just turned eleven and now she could attend youth group. She had daydreamed about being a part of the youth group since her family first started to attend the church. The youth would always sit in the back of the church, in their own little group. They looked so cool. Karrie smiled at herself in the mirror. She didn't quite look like a teen yet, but things were changing, she could feel it in her body. She bent her head forward and brushed her orange hair from the back over her sunburnt, freckled face; then she turned her head upright and tried to style her stiff, frizzy curls like the lady's in the hair spray commercial. Then she grabbed her Bible and flung open her bedroom door, moving as quickly as she could, but quietly so she would not wake her father. She darted toward the front door.

Then it happened. A big fleshy arm slammed the door shut again.

"Where ya going? Twit!"

Pete, her older brother, leaned against the front door with his arms folded across his puffed-up chest. His face was hard and angry. His face was always angry.

"I'm going to church. Mama said I could go to church today." Karrie backed up so she could be just outside of the grasp of Pete's fist in case he decided to take a swing at her.

"Nope, it's Wednesday and not Sunday, so you're not going anywhere!"

Karrie's face flushed; she could feel the tears in the corner of her eyes but held them back by gritting her teeth so her brother wouldn't see any weakness. "I'm going to youth group." She looked past her brother toward the locked door and tried to make her face as hard as her brother's.

"Nope, I'm in charge now. Mom's working the afternoon shift, so you gotta do what I say now."

Just then, Karrie could hear the back door swing open, and her brother Andrew ran in.

"Hey Pete . . . " Andrew ran into the middle of the living room and stood between Pete and Karrie. "That old sick possum just crawled out from the canyon!"

"Sick!" yelled Pete. He pushed Karrie aside and ran toward the back door. Karrie and Andrew locked eyes in mutual approval. She smiled at Andrew and then darted out the front door and down the street to the church.

Karrie's church was an ivory stucco building designed to look like the old Spanish adobe buildings that were built in California and Mexico a century ago. It had the metal cross on top of the red tile roof. Her church was the most beautiful building in the whole world. It stood like a powerful tower in the middle of her neighborhood, above the smaller Spanish-style houses and apartment buildings.

The little church meant so many things she could not explain them in words. She loved the smell of the perfume on all the ladies in church, the swell of organ music that echoed inside the sanctuary walls, and the hugs that awaited her on the church patio during coffee hour. That church was the hope of Karrie's world.

"Miss Dawn!" she shouted from across the street when she saw her Sunday school teacher. "Miss Dawn, can I walk with you?"

"Well, I don't see anyone else walking with me, so sure, Karrie, I would love to have your company." Miss Dawn was a tall, slender woman in her mid-twenties, but Karrie thought she looked like a teenager. Miss Dawn had long blonde hair that fell gracefully around her face and cascaded down her back as if being blown by an unseen wind.

As they were crossing the street, Karrie realized her teacher was walking toward the front of the church. "No! Don't turn here!" Karrie cried out when they got to the corner. "Let's go through the side door. I've got something to show the pastor."

"Goodness, Karrie, calm down. What do you mean hollering at me in front of the church like that?"

Miss Dawn's voice sounded sharp, so Karrie squeezed her hand and yanked on it slightly so Miss Dawn would lower her head so Karrie could whisper in her ear. "I want to show Pastor Will something. Let's walk around the other way so we can pass by his office. We can come in the side door of the church."

Karrie pulled Miss Dawn toward the left side of the church. As they turned the corner, a blast of hot summer wind hit Karrie's face. Her heart skipped a beat when she saw the silhouettes of Pastor Will and his wife in the sunset standing by the church's side steps. She ran up to him and started to pull her hand out of her pocket to show him her splinter but stopped when she saw three other girls from her Sunday school class sitting on the stairs together in front of Pastor Will.

Mrs. Anderson was standing by the girls, proudly gazing down on them.

"Yes, Pastor Will, it was Anna's tenth birthday, so I thought I'd treat her to her first manicure." Mrs. Anderson smiled down at the three girls beaming up at her and the pastor. All three girls sat with hands held out in front of them. Six hands with perfectly shell-like rounded nails glistening in the sun. Bright pink, pearly green, and pale purple nails graced each of their hands. Each nail tip sparkled with silver glitter.

"Pastor," said Miss Dawn as they reached the church steps. "Karrie has something to show you."

REV. CHERYL ANNE KINCAID   13

Karrie's face warmed with embarrassment. "No, I don't," she said. She shoved her hand back into her pocket.

"Now, Karrie, you just told me you had something to share with Pastor Will—what's wrong with you now? Why are you suddenly so shy?"

"I forgot what it was," stammered Karrie. "We're going to be late for church."

Pastor Will put his hand on Karrie's head. His hand on her head felt like a kind hug. "Karrie, I'd be happy to hear what you have to share with me when you remember. But Karrie is right. We're going to be late—you for the youth group and me for the prayer meeting. The sun is already setting."

The three girls got up and brushed themselves off and walked toward the church gym's front door. They were followed by Pastor Will and Mrs. Anderson; Miss Dawn and Karrie followed them.

"Karrie," whispered Miss Dawn. "What's wrong?"

"Nothing," said Karrie. "I thought I knew something, and then I realized I didn't. Just forget it, please." She pulled on Miss Dawn's arm again so she could whisper in her ear. "Miss Dawn, why did Jesus still have sores on His hands after He rose from the dead?"

Miss Dawn's forehead winkled, and she looked down at Karrie the same way Grandma had looked at her. Karrie hated that look. She was familiar with it. It was the look grown-ups gave her when they were trying to figure her out. It seemed as though every grown-up she had ever known had looked at her that way.

"Karrie, your mind goes in twelve different directions at once. Wow! What a question!" Miss Dawn leaned against the wall and put her arm around Karrie. "Well, first of all, they were scars and not sores," Miss Dawn corrected her.

"Okay. Scars, then," Karrie said impatiently. "I wanted to show Pastor something—something that was like what he said in his sermon." Karrie's voice began to tremble.

"Child, you're getting yourself all upset over nothing," Miss Dawn said.

"No," protested Karrie, "it's something. At least it's something to *me*. I was thinking about Pastor's sermon last week, when Thomas asked to see Jesus's sores—I mean scars. Why did Jesus still have them if He was healed and all that?"

Miss Dawns face wrinkled again, and Karrie's face warmed again in embarrassment.

"I thought that maybe because Jesus had scars, maybe we should want them, too."

"Karrie, I can't seem to figure out what you are trying to say to me." Miss Dawn brushed Karrie's hair away from her forehead.

The youth pastor opened the doors to the gym, and Karrie could hear the squeals of teenage laughter and the pounding feet of kids running across the gym. She saw her friends in one corner of the room.

"Never mind," Karrie said, breaking away from Miss Dawn's arms. She ran into the youth center and found her friends. Somewhere in the middle of the smiles, whispers about cute boys, and inside jokes, Karrie forgot about her splinter; and her embarrassed face cooled in the sound of laughter.

Chapter 2

"Karrie, are you comin'?" Karrie's mom swung the large laundry basket onto her hip while she opened the front door.

"I'm comin'. I'm just trying to get rest of the coins from the bottom of the drawer." Karrie had pulled the large kitchen drawer out as far as it could go. She rested the junk-filled drawer on one knee as she dug through bills, papers, rubber bands, and coupons to find coins for the laundromat. Today was the first Saturday of the month, and it was laundry day. Karrie was scooping out the quarters and dimes that had been saved from the previous week's grocery market change. Now her pockets were heavy with coins. She crammed the drawer back into its place and ran into the bathroom to get the basket cart of dirty clothes. She rolled the cart through the living room and out the front door where her mother was waiting on the porch.

When she walked outside, a light wind cooled her face and fluttered through her hair, blowing it off her face.

"Now didn't that breeze feel nice?" Mama smiled and put down the laundry basket she was carrying. She steadied Karrie's cart with one hand while firmly pushing the clothes down so they would all fit. "Karrie, pull it behind you. That will steady the cart and keep the clothes from falling out."

She picked up her basket, and they both began their three-block walk to the laundromat. Karrie liked these walks with her mother. Even when they didn't talk, they were good walks.

It was a beautiful day. For a while, no one said anything. But there was a storm brewing inside of Karrie; and today she knew she had to say something. "Mama," she said as they were leaving the house. "I think Dad's been drinking again."

"I think he's just tired, Karrie. He's been looking for a job for some time now." Karrie's mother let out a sigh. "Don't be so quick to judge."

Karrie looked down at the ground, watching her feet as they started to walk up the hill. She was quiet for a long time; she didn't want to say anything more about it. Talking about her father made her stomach hurt, and it made her mom scream, and Karrie hated it when her mom screamed at her. But she could hear an alarm sounding off inside her, and she couldn't hold it in, so she blurted out, "He smelled like booze yesterday when I came home from Grandma's."

"Karrie, are we going to argue the whole walk today? Let's talk about something more pleasant." Karrie's mom was quiet for a while, and then she said, "Grandma said you got a splinter in your hand on Wednesday, and you wouldn't let her take it out. What's that all about?"

"It's nothing, Mama." She looked up from the ground. They were at the street corner now. Karrie could see the heat rising from the black pavement into mysterious ripples in the air. For a moment, the black tar street looked almost liquid. She tenuously put her foot on the street. She imagined for a moment her foot might sink through the soft black tar and she would discover the pavement was really fudge and not a tar-paved road at all. But then her foot landed solidly on hard tar street. *Screeeech*!

A car squealed to a stop a few feet from Karrie, and a red-faced man stuck his face outside the car window and yelled. "Stupid kid, what you think you're doing? You going to get yourself killed. Hey lady, watch your kid!"

Karrie looked up at her mom's red frowning face. "I'm sorry, Mama."

Karrie's mom waited for the car to speed away before she said, "You got to look where you're going."

"But he shouldn't have been driving so fast. This is still a residential neighborhood with a school down the street even if we are near a freeway. People like him are just trying to speed through our neighborhood to get to the freeway, but this road isn't the freeway. I bet he doesn't drive that way on the street where his kids play."

They were quiet for the rest of the walk to the laundromat. "Here we are, almost without incident," Mama said when they arrived.

The laundromat's walls were painted bright yellow with sponge-printed orange sunflowers sprinkled across them. The sound of the spinning washers and dryers roared like the ocean. The room smelled of lilac detergent and fabric softener.

Karrie and Mama had a plan on afternoons when the laundromat was full. Karrie would find an empty space on the long white counter in the middle of the floor for sorting clothes, while Mama would find two or three washers and dryers together for their loads. Karrie found a space near the end of the long white counter for their clothes and then stepped up on one of the white plastic chairs and began to pull the clothes out of her wheeled cart she had been pulling and put them on the counter. Mama found two washers next to each other and set two chairs in front of them, in hopes no one would move them until they were ready to put their clothes into them. Then she joined Karrie at the counter and dumped out her basket of clothes next to Karrie's. She made two piles of clothing—one dark pile and one light. They smiled triumphantly at each other at their ability to implement their plan so quickly. They dug into their chore, separating light from dark and pulling out stained or torn garments into a separate pile.

"Ma'am, are you going to be using those two washers?"

Karrie looked up and saw a tall marine in compact clothes carrying a large duffel over his shoulder. "Well, we're ready for one of them, at least." Karrie's mother scooped up a pile of white laundry in her arms. "But I guess you can have the other one. Karrie, can you get the door of the washer for me?"

Karrie ran over to the washer, but the marine beat her. He stood in front of her and, with his large muscular arm, pulled open the washer door. Across his arm was a tattoo of Christ on the cross with His head stretched out by the muscles on the man's arm.

"That's some tattoo," Mama said as she heaved the load of laundry into the washer.

"Yeah," said the marine. "I got it in basic training three years ago. I got it when I was baptized before we were shipped out. Chaplain said the tattoo was more Catholic than Protestant because Jesus was still on the cross. But I like it better."

"Because Jesus looks tougher," Karrie interrupted.

"Karrie! Don't interrupt," Mama scolded as she poured the detergent into the washer.

"No," said the marine, "she's right. After the stuff I saw, I like it better."

"Well, we got to get back to our sorting, and I'm sure you've got things to do, too." Mama nodded her head toward the overstuffed duffle bag. She put her hand on Karrie's back and led her back to the counter.

"Mama," Karrie said after a moment of silent sorting, "do you remember the sermon Sunday?"

"Not word for word, but I think I got the gist of it," Mama said.

"It bothered me that Pastor Will said that Jesus still had His sores—I mean scars—after He rose from the dead."

"Why did that bother you, Karrie?" Mama asked while pulling another pile of clothing toward her.

"Because He didn't have to have them after He visited God in heaven. So why, Mama? Why did Jesus still have scars on His hands when He came back from the dead?" The whole time Karrie was talking, she was trying to untwist a pair of leggings from a purple sweatshirt.

"Karrie Heppuch Leary, I will never understand how your mind works," Mama said as she put her hands on her hips and shook her head while looking down at Karrie. At first, she seemed angry at the question, and then she broke out laughing. Mama's laugh broke through the tension of the day, and Karrie joined her. "Girl, give me those knotted clothes. You're just making it worse." Mama shook out both twisted pieces of clothing; the knot loosened, and the clothes separated. "You don't ask the same the questions most kids do. Do you know that?" Mama asked with a chuckle.

"But don't you remember Pastor Will's sermon last week? When the disciple Thomas asked to see Jesus's scars? So why did Jesus still have them if God had made Him all better?"

Mama picked up an armful of dark clothing and motioned for Karrie to pick up the load of light clothing to put into two washers that had become available across the room. "I don't know." Mama sighed. "Maybe it was just to prove that He was alive again."

"But, Mama, Thomas seeing Jesus again would prove He was alive again. Thomas didn't have to see the scars. And I don't think any of the disciples would mistake Jesus for anyone else, because you know, He was Jesus. So, Jesus didn't need the scars to prove He was Jesus, so why would Jesus keep His scars?"

"Karrie, that's enough!" Mama closed her eyes and talked slowly, putting emphasis on each word she said to let Karrie know this was the end of this conversation. She motioned for Karrie to pick up the box of laundry detergent still on the counter. Mama poured a cup of detergent into each of the washers. "Karrie, the pastor was talking about doubting. Thomas saw Jesus, and he stopped doubting, and that is all there is to say about it. You're always making more of something than there really is. Now let's talk about something else."

"Mama, can I get my nails done at one of the beauty shops?" Karrie blurted out.

Mama smiled again. "Now that sounds more like a question I can handle." She sat down in a white chair next to their washers and said, "No, honey, we don't have the money for one of those manicure shops, and I don't have extra grocery money to spend on nail polish."

"But Mama can't someone in your shop at work do my nails?" Karrie asked.

"We don't do nails at my small shop, Karrie. And even if we did, I'd have to pay someone to do your nails and the money is just not there." Mama's face softened when she saw Karrie look down. She tilted up Karrie's chin so they were face-to-face. "But I'll tell ya what, Aunt Mary left some makeup samples from the store for me. You can have whatever is there."

"Mama," Karrie smiled as they each put the last armful of clothing in the washers—"why'd you name me Karrie Heppuch?"

Mama shook her head again. She looked down at Karrie and nodded toward Karrie's pockets. Karrie reached into her pockets and scooped out a handful of silver coins. Mama took three quarters and two dimes to put in the washers.

"Tell me again, Mama. Why?" Karrie asked as she put her coins into the washer next to her.

"Stop fishing for compliments, Karrie." She put her last coin into one of the washers and walked toward the white plastic chairs under the front window in the Laundromat. "You already know why I named you Karrie."

"Tell me again, please," Karrie whined.

Mama smiled, and she sat down in the first white chair by the door, where they both could feel the summer breeze. Then she pulled Karrie near her and wrapped her arm around her. "Things used to be good between your daddy and me. Then things got worse with the drinking and other things. So I went to church, and the preacher talked about Job's daughters, the ones who were born out of adversity. By that, I mean after his trials. He said Job's middle daughter was named Karrie Heppuch, which meant the incense used in prayer. So she was kind of an answer to his prayers. And something in that sermon made sense to me. I still can't say all of what it meant to me, but something inside of me got brave because of that sermon. I found out I was pregnant the Monday after that sermon, so I named you Karrie Heppuch—because you were the answer to my prayer to God." Mama squeezed her tight.

Chapter 3

Karrie rose the next morning an hour earlier. She had found Aunt Mary's store samples under Mama's sewing drawer. There were no nail polish samples, but there were six different colors of tiny lipstick samples. She carefully took out the tiny lipsticks. She would color all her nails pink, but every other nail would be light pink. With the tiny samples, she carefully lined the inside rim of each of her nails and then filled them in with small strokes of pink color. She found some glitter in the bottom of the drawer and lightly sprinkled each nail with gold glitter. Then she carefully slipped her sweater over her arm, curling her fingers into a half fist so the lipstick would not smudge off. She pushed her back against the front door so she wouldn't smudge her lipstick nails.

Karrie's brother was waiting for her on the porch. "Come on, Karrie, we're going to miss the bus!" Andrew grabbed her arm, and Karrie pulled it back.

"Wait a minute. I need to make sure my backpack is zipped up." Karrie looked down at her nails. *Good!* They had not gotten smeared. She zipped up her bag and then flung it over her shoulder and ran outside to join her brother.

"You don't think, Karrie, that's the problem?" Andrew asked as he passed her by, walking ahead of her. His legs were so long his small steps were Karrie's big steps.

"What do ya mean?" She picked up her stride as if to try to keep up with her brother.

"I mean Pete. You don't keep out of his away. That's why he always picks on you. When he walks in the room, you got to just walk out. Avoid him."

"I do, but he always finds me. He's always mad at me."

By this time, they had reached the bus stop. Andrew smiled at Karrie. "Chin up, kid. You're better than him. You know that, don't you?" Then he yelled over his shoulder to her as he ran toward the corner where his friends were waiting in a tight cluster. "Stay away from him!"

"The house isn't that big," Karrie whispered to herself as her brother left her. "The world isn't that big." Karrie saw the yellow bus turn slowly around the corner.

It rolled to a squeaky stop and heaved a giant sigh as it slowed in front of her and opened its huge, collapsing door. Karrie had butterflies in her stomach; she saw the faces of all the children leaning out the windows. She felt ready to make her entrance. She heaved her backpack onto her shoulder, making sure her pink nails rested on the outside of the backpack. The boys piled on to the bus first, and they were greeted with cheers. Then the older kids climbed on and found their favorite seats.

Karrie poked her head inside the bus door before she got on. She could see the four girls from church sitting in the second row of seats on the bus. All of them had on purple tank tops, and perfectly rounded polka dot shell necklaces and silver-beaded bracelets. Then it was Karrie's turn to get on the bus. She grabbed the metal handle on the side of bus's steps as she pulled herself up. She smiled and tried to pretend she had just finished laughing at some joke told to her by an unseen friend. Karrie walked slowly by the second row, making sure the girls from church saw her colored nails resting on her backpack. She sat down in the fourth row. She glanced down at her nails; her entrance was a success. Her nails had not smudged. Then she looked up and saw Mona coming toward her.

Mona's father owned the drugstore near the church. He always seemed kind, but Mona didn't seem to know how to be kind. Mona was always smiling, but her face was hard, especially when she looked at Karrie. "Hey, Kar, I like your skirt." Mona moved to the seat next to hers.

"Thanks. My mom got it for me." Karrie rested her hands on the chair in front of her so the sun from the window would bounce off the glitter on her nails.

"I know," said Mona. "It was my skirt. My grandma made it for me, and I hated the color, so she gave it to your mom. You know we were just doing what Jesus would do—helping out the poor and all that." Mona's words sounded sweet, but they pierced Karrie's heart. How could words be sweet and mean at the same time? "Like your nails—did you get your nails painted?" Mona asked.

"Yeah," said Karrie. "My mom took me to that fancy shop, too."

Mona wiped her thumb over Karrie's hand, and the lipstick smeared off. "Oooh, what's on your nails? It's gooey!" This time Mona raised her voice so the whole bus could hear her.

Karrie tried to stop from blushing, but her face turned red anyway. Karrie forced a smile and tried to laugh. "It was just a joke. I wanted to see if I could fool ya. It's lipstick. My mom's going to take me to that nail place tomorrow."

"It's a gross joke," said Mona. "But I'll tell ya what, you go there tomorrow, and we'll have a contest to see which one of us has the prettiest nails next Wednesday night at the church, okay?"

"Yeah, okay." Karrie turned up the corners of her mouth into a smile. She could feel warm tears forming in the corners of her eyes, but she made her face hard so she could hold them back. She put her hands on her lap and wiped off the rest of lipstick she had worked so hard at applying to her nails that morning.

"It's okay, Karrie. They're just mean," a voice said from behind her.

It was Scott. He went to Karrie's church, too. Scott had Down Syndrome, and Karrie would talk to him at church all the time, but she didn't want to talk to him now. All the adults seemed to take care of Scott at church; he was loved at church, but at school, he was teased. She didn't want to be mean, but she was scared of being called weird. She turned around to see if there was a seat by her brother. She tried to get up to move, but Scott put his hand over her hands. His hands were heavy and warm, and his grasp felt kind and somehow it was helping her to hold back her tears. Scott's hands felt the same as Pastor Will's hand had felt on her head yesterday.

Scott smiled and Karrie smiled, and she didn't change her seat. Somehow, Scott's smile cooled her embarrassment.

Chapter 4

When Karrie got home, she saw Mama and Aunt Mary on the front porch. Aunt Mary was leaning against the wall, and Mama was sitting in the wicker chair on the porch with her head in her hands.

"Mama, what's wrong," Karrie asked.

"Nothing, honey," Mama said while she wiped her eyes. She looked at Karrie and then back at Aunt Mary. "Seems like last week that I brought her home from the hospital."

"Seems that way to me, too," Aunt Mary said. "My, what a big schoolgirl you look like now, Karrie."

"I'm going to be in middle school next year," said Karrie, smiling.

"Boy, time sure passes, don't it," Aunt Mary said. "Now, your Mama's been telling me there's some kind of contest at church about painted nails?"

"Yeah, Aunt Mary. Do you have any polish?" asked Karrie.

"I might. I am going to go visit Grandma. If you come with me, I might find time to paint your nails."

Karrie ran up to her aunt and hugged her.

"Now let's go for a ride to Grandma's house," said Aunt Mary. Then she looked up at Mama. "Are you going to be all right?"

"Sure," said Mama. "It's not that big of a deal."

Karrie looked up at her mother and saw for the first time that her mother's left eye was swollen. "Oh, Mama," she gasped.

"Mountains out of molehills, Karrie," said Mama. "It's no big deal. You go over to your grandma and enjoy the day with your aunt. I'll be fine."

Karrie stomach began to hurt, but she did what she was told and walked over to Aunt Mary's car.

Aunt Mary didn't bring Karrie home until after five. From the car they could hear her mother and father yelling at each other. Aunt Mary frowned when she looked out the car window, and Karrie felt flush with embarrassment."Maybe you can stay with me or Grandma tonight, Karrie?" Aunt Mary said.

"No. I want to go home. It'll be okay in an hour or so. Don't worry about it, Aunt Mary." She kissed her aunt and then got out of the car.

Aunt Mary drove slowly away, looking over her shoulder at the small tan house. Karrie walked around the house to the back garage. She had kept two coffee cans by the garage door beside the alley. This was where she kept her treasures. In one can, she had a dried sunflower from Grandma's garden, a pair of rainbow-colored dragonfly wings, a rice bag from Miss Dawn's wedding, and a glow-in-the-dark plastic cross she had won at church for memorizing the Twenty-third Psalm. The other can was full of seashells and colored rocks she collected each time she had gone to the beach with the church. She picked up her shell-filled can and squatted in a corner of the garage. She poured out the shells all over the floor; they fell into an ivory-colored little hill. She did a final shake of the can, and a black beetle and two brown roaches fell out after the shells. The bugs crawled over the small hill of shells and disappeared into a dark corner of the garage. She picked out ten yellowed pinkish half shells from the small hill of shells. She washed them off with water from the faucet on the side of the garage. She held the shells in her hand, and the water made them shine in the afternoon sun.

"Karrie."

The sound of Andrew's voice made her jump, and she dropped the shells on the ground.

"What are you doing out here?"

"I'm not doing anything." Karrie scooped up the shells from the floor and shoved them in her pocket. "What are you doing here?" she asked.

"I'm supposed to sweep out the garage," Andrew said, looking around for the outside broom. "I thought I'd do that now so I could get out of the house."

"Why?" asked Karrie. "What's going on?"

"Mom and Dad are fighting. Dad's been drinking, and you know the rest. I hate it when they scream at each other." Andrew had now found the broom in corner of the garage and started to twirl it around over his head. There was a long moment of heavy silence; they both watched the broom while Andrew twirled it in fast circles as it whisked through the summer air.

Then Karrie spoke. "Andrew, can I borrow some of your airplane glue you got for Christmas?"

"I guess," he said as he started to push the broom across the floor. "What do you want it for?"

"I'm going to make a shell necklace," Karrie said as she reached into her back pocket and pulled out a long piece of string. "I got some string from Mom's old macramé kit. I braided it together and then turned it over and braided it again." She bent down and scooped up a handful of shells she had dropped on the ground. She opened her hand and held out the shells to show them to Andrew, and she smiled looking up at him as if she was holding a handful of pearls. "I'm going to glue shells on each side of the string to make a necklace."

"I don't think they will hold together, Kar," Andrew said, "The shells are too heavy. The string will break."

"Maybe not," Karrie said, turning her hand toward the sun so the shells would glisten again.

Andrew shook his head. "It won't work, Karrie. Besides, you don't have a jewelry clasp. How are you going to hold the necklace together?"

"I'm going tie them in a knot in the back."

"How?" Andrew asked. "What kind of knot are you going to make? You can't make it a slipknot, or you'll choke yourself. If you make it a square knot, it'll pull so tight you won't be able to untie it. So you'll have to break the string every time you take it off. After a while, it will get so small you won't be able to put it around your neck."

"I don't care. I just want to wear it once on Wednesday," mumbled Karrie.

Andrew looked Karrie straight in the eye. "You mean for that stupid contest?"

"What contest? How do you know about any contest?"

"The whole bus heard you on Monday, Kar." Andrew started to push the broom across the floor.

"It's not a stupid contest! Aunt Mary painted my nails tonight, see?" Karrie held up her hands to show him her five pink-tipped nails. "They look good."

"They don't look like they were done at the nail place, Karrie."

"It's none of your business anyway," Karrie said as she shoved her hands back into her pockets.

"Why do you do stuff like that?" Andrew asked while sweeping up the dust into a small pile of brown dirt on the garage floor.

"Hey, watch out! You're gonna break my shells!" Karrie shouted as she squatted down and began to scoop her pile of shells back into her coffee can.

"Those girls are never going to like you, Karrie. It doesn't matter what you do."

"So? I don't care. I just want to make a necklace." Karrie stood up again and looked at her brother. "Can I borrow the glue or not?"

"Yeah, you can borrow it." Andrew sighed. "It's in our bedroom." Andrew and their brother Pete shared a bedroom. Karrie turned to run toward her brothers' room.

"No, Karrie!" her brother yelled. He lowered his voice as Karrie walked back. "Don't go in there. If Pete's in there after Dad's been with him, he'll take it out on you! I'll get you the glue later, and then you give it back to me when you're done. Do you hear me? I don't want Pete to catch you. And don't tell Pete I gave it to you. He gets mad when I give things to you."

"I hear you," she said quietly. She looked over her shoulder at the house. "Do you think it's safe to go in yet?"

"Yeah, I heard Dad drive away a while ago. Mom's probably crying in her room. I'll make you some oatmeal for dinner."

"Thanks, Andy," Karrie said.

Andrew rubbed Karrie's head, messing up her hair, and she smiled at her brother.

Chapter 5

Seven shells made a small rippled line on the placemat in the corner of the table. After dinner the night before, she had placed seven shells in a row across her placemat. She carefully took off the cap on the airplane glue and put a small drop into each of the curved centers of the shells. She laid the braided string in a line over the shells. She chose seven more shells. She placed a small drop of glue in each of those shells and placed them on top of the others with the string resting between them.

It was now Wednesday evening, an hour before youth group. She carefully held up the string of shells, and the necklace held together. When she held it up to the light, the shells showed their different colors; in the garage, they all looked the same. Some shells were slightly more yellow or pink than the others, but together, they were all a pale ivory color. Today, next to the living room light and glued together on the string, no shell seemed to be the same color as the other. On one shell, she saw blue hues and purple shadows. On others, she saw red and gray lines that ran across some of them. Others had yellowed sunsets that rested in the corners. She held it up proudly and smiled, staring at her necklace. She placed the necklace around her neck and tied a small square knot on the back of it, just under her hairline, on her nape.

"Hey, what are ya doing with Andrew's glue?" Pete yelled from behind her.

Karrie startled at the sound and turned around and saw Pete. Parts of his red hair stood up on their ends as if his night sweat had dried and stiffened his hair. Karrie gasped when she saw his face. His left eye had a red halo that even at this very moment had begun to turn brown in the corners. On his left arm, she could see the five reddish-purple imprints of her father's hand that had left their mark.

"Oh, Pete," Karrie gasped. "I'm so sorry."

"What!" Pete screamed. "You, sorry for me! What? Who are you to be sorry for anyone?" Pete began to mutter a string of names and words that garbled together in Karrie's head.

She couldn't fully understand all the words, but she knew he was angry, and she was frightened. She turned and grabbed her Bible and quickened her pace toward the door. If she could reach the church, where people were standing out front, she knew he wouldn't be able to hit her in front of them. Karrie walked down the street.

She tried to smile, to pretend that Pete wasn't behind her, swearing at her. Adults from cars passing by looked out their windows at her brother and her with confused stares.

Karrie reached the corner where she could see the church, standing there in all its glory. She felt safe now. Maybe Pete would stop when he saw the church people out in front. Maybe he would turn around and leave her alone. In the center of the patio, there were the four girls from her Sunday school class and Mrs. Anderson. Miss Dawn and the pastor were talking, standing off to the side of the girls. Other church members gathered in clusters laughing, talking, and moving gracefully about in the summer evening air.

"Hey everyone," Karrie shouted when she saw the Pastor and Miss Dawn. She tried her hardest to force a smile.

It seemed as if everyone on the patio turned and looked at Karrie and her brother in his rage behind her. Then everyone stopped talking; no one was smiling. Pete's profane words silenced all of them. They stood there with their mouths wide open but no words coming out. Karrie wanted to make a joke, to say something to make the situation more bearable.

Then it happened—the thing that Karrie feared most. She felt the powerful blow of her brother's foot on her back. It flung her forward and face down onto the ground. The macramé rope around her neck broke, and her shells flew into the air across the church patio. Some shells bounced, others shattered into pieces, other smashed when they hit the ground and crumbled into white dust. Karrie picked herself up and wiped her face and saw a red smear of blood from her cut lip.

"Karrie!" Pastor Will yelled. He ran across the patio toward Karrie and her brother. "You, young man, you stay where you are," Pastor Will yelled at Pete.

"No!" screamed Karrie. "Don't hurt him!" She tried to pick herself up, but her body froze in pain and shame. Pastor Will knelt beside her, and she whispered to him through her tears. "He didn't kick me because he's mean, but he did because he's just embarrassed, and he's angry."

He gently put his hand behind her back supporting her as she sat up. "Dad hurts him, and he can't be angry at Dad, because Dad is Dad," Karrie said as Pastor Will helped her to turn, "so he gets angry at me. He's just embarrassed, you see. He knows things at our house aren't right, and he can't change them, so instead he joins them so no one will be mad at Mom and Dad." Karrie spoke between sobs that she could not hold back.

Karrie's last words seemed to make the whole world stop. No one moved on the church patio; they all stood frozen like statues. Karrie had spoken a truth everyone already knew but no one wanted to say.

"Did you figure that out all by yourself, Karrie?" whispered Pastor Will.

"It didn't take that much figuring," said Karrie. She sat for a moment and closed her eyes and felt the summer wind cool her face. "So please don't be angry at him, Pastor. It'll just hurt him more." Karrie sobbed freely and then felt the gentle hands of Miss Dawn, who helped her to her feet. Miss Dawn held her up as she walked her across the church patio into the safety of her Sunday school classroom.

Chapter 6

Karrie sat down in her favorite chair in the Sunday school classroom. Miss Dawn went to the classroom sink and pulled out a paper towel from the art supplies cabinet and ran cool water over it. She sat next to Karrie and gave it to her.

Karrie pressed the cool paper towel against her warm face. "Karrie," Miss Dawn said, "do you want to talk to me about what just happened out there?"

Karrie shook her head and looked at the ground.

"You know, Karrie, you asked me a question yesterday, and I didn't answer it. But I've been thinking a lot about it. Do you remember the question you asked about Jesus's scars?"

While Miss Dawn was talking, she reached into her purse and pulled out sanitary wipe in a plastic bag. She opened the bag and unfolded the napkin. She gently opened Karrie's hands and began to wipe the dirt away. "You know, there's a lot of pain in this world, and it leaves a lot of scars—more than any of us would like to know about. There are a lot of the people in this world that seem to suffer for no reason," Miss Dawn whispered as she washed Karrie's face and placed a cold towel on her lip. Then she washed Karrie's thumb. Miss Dawn took out a pair of tweezers from of her purse. "There are so many tears so deep that many people just stop crying because they are frightened that if they start, they will never stop."

With her tweezers, Miss Dawn grasped the end of Karrie's splinter and yanked it out. A red pearl of blood rolled down Karrie's arm. Miss Dawn placed a cotton ball dipped in cool antibiotic gel over the wound. "There are people in this world that seem to suffer for nothing, but Jesus, He didn't suffer for nothing. He suffered for something. He carried a lot more on that cross than just our sin. He carried, and still carries, our tears, too."

Miss Dawn's voice was soft and comforting, and Karrie's head began to feel heavy. She leaned over to lay her head on Miss Dawn's shoulder as hot, round tears that had been held back for days rolled uncontrollably down Karrie's cheeks. While she cried, Miss Dawn smoothed her hair. "And I believe that is why Jesus kept His scars. I think it was to show us that we are not alone when we cry or when it hurts so bad that we cannot cry."

Miss Dawn began to rock Karrie to calm her down. "I think Thomas needed to see those scars, because he had his own scars. It was enough for the other disciples just to see Jesus's face, but Thomas needed to see the Jesus who died on the cross. It was only Jesus's scars that could heal Thomas's scars."

As Miss Dawn talked, Karrie cried for the men with tired faces by the liquor stores. She cried because of the soured wine on her father's breath, and she cried for Pete's bruises. She cried for teenagers with hard faces on the street corners, and she cried because her grandma would never own a long silk dress with golden roses embroidered on the collar. She cried because she could never be the answer to her mother's prayers. And while Miss Dawn stroked her hair, Karrie could feel Pastor Will's hand and Scott's smile and the arms of everyone at church who had ever hugged her. And like Thomas, two thousand years ago, she felt she was reaching up to touch the scars in Jesus's hands.

Chapter 7

The sky had turned from a light blue with orange sunset streaks into the dark blue of early evening when Karrie and Miss Dawn walked back onto the church patio. Rays of blue and red light shot across the patio from the top of a police car parked in front of the church. Pastor Will was standing next to Pete, his arm around Pete's shoulder.

Pete's face wasn't hard as usual; in fact, the look on it was soft like a child's as he talked to a police officer, who knelt in front of him while writing something down in a small notebook. All four girls from Karrie's Sunday school class watched Karrie as she walked out with Miss Dawn. Mona was standing next to her father, his arm around her, and her head leaned against his chest. Her face wasn't hard anymore either; her face was soft and red with tear stains on her cheeks. She no longer looked like a schoolyard bully but more like a lost child who had just found her way home.

"You okay, Karrie?" asked Jennifer, who stood in the center of the cluster and had her arms around her mother.

Karrie nodded and tried to turn the corners of her mouth upward into a half smile.

"I'm sorry," said Mona, "about the nail polish and the stupid idea of a contest. I don't know why I do stuff like that."

"What contest?" Pastor Will had now joined the cluster.

"Our hands," said Karrie. "We all got our nails polished, and we were going see who had the prettiest hands. See?"

Karrie started to hold up her hands to show the pink nail polish, but then she remembered the big white Band-Aid on her thumb.

"Now that doesn't sound like a half-bad idea." Pastor Will smiled as he held out his hands. "Come on, let's all put out our hands."

Each of the girls put out their hands into the circle, but in the night air, the nail polish color had dimmed. The only thing that shone bright was the white cotton ball with white tape Miss Dawn had put on Karrie's thumb.

"Who has the prettiest hands, Miss Dawn?" asked Pastor Will.

"I guess we can't know that until we see what those hands do," she replied.

"I think the most useful thing God gives us are our hands," Pastor Will said as he held up his hands and turned them around. "I see some hands that are able to do some great works of kindness. I see some hands that can inflict pain as well. I guess we're just going to have to wait and see what these hands can do before we know which hand will create the most beauty."

Somewhere in the middle of Pastor Will's speech, the girls' hands moved from the middle of the circle to around each other's backs. As the summer wind blew in and around that circle, Karrie felt she could smell Grandma's garden. Only, this wind smelled more beautiful and richer as if it had come from a closer place. Karrie wondered if this small circle was surrounded by the aroma from the same garden she had heard about in Sunday school, where God had walked in the cool of the day with His children.

> *How beautiful are the feet of those who bring good news!*
> —Romans 10:15

Chapter 8

Streams of blue, yellow, and red blurred together through the raindrop-spattered windshield of the police car.

"What ya staring at, Karrie?" Andrew asked. His cold stare was more than Karrie could bear.

Andrew had been quiet for the whole drive. After the police had questioned Karrie and Pete at the church, they found Andrew in the canyon playing with his friends. A light-green Honda driven by a policewoman with kind eyes arrived at the church with Andrew in the back seat. She opened the door, and Andrew stepped out of the car, his face white and serious.

Karrie had never seen him look that way before. When she saw Andrew, she ran toward him, expecting to get a hug, or perhaps for him to mess up her hair with his knuckles while making a funny remark. Instead, he stepped away from her, and he stared so coldly it broke her heart.

The policeman motioned for them both to get in the back seat of the police car. The policewoman walked across the church patio to where Pete was still talking to the other officer. Pete's face was wrinkled up and red. He was shaking, and his chest was heaving up and down as if it was painful for him to breathe. His eyes were darting from side to side so he could look up and down the block. He was talking so fast in whimpering tones as if he were a lost dog that was trapped and crying out for his owner.

In all her life, Karrie had never seen Pete cry. Now, he looked as if he wished he could cry, but no tears came out of his eyes; he just pleaded in a high-pitched voice.

The policewoman bent down and put her hand on Pete's shoulders and talked quietly to him. He seemed to calm down. She pointed toward her car, turned, and walked toward the car. Pete followed the policewoman to the car. She opened the door to the back seat, and he got in, and they drove away.

Karrie and Andrew sat like strangers in the back of the police car. Andrew was so quiet she couldn't even hear his breathing. Two police officers, a man and a woman, climbed into the front seat. When the policeman turned on the ignition, the sky crackled with the sound of thunder, and a streak of lightning pierced the gray sky. The sky opened, and big, round raindrops broke through and pounded the police car from every side.

Karrie thought the sky was crying the tears that Pete could not. As they entered the freeway, the rain stopped, and Karrie saw a rainbow resting in the white-and-gray-lined clouds. It absorbed all her attention.

"What ya staring at, Karrie?" Andrew asked.

Karrie's heart skipped a beat at the sound of Andrew's voice. Now he was talking to her again. "The rainbow—remember when we were kids and I thought that a rainbow happened because the clouds were reflecting the color of the oil and the car grease in the streets?"

Karrie smiled and moved closer to Andrew, but Andrew's face was still cold. "Well, it's not true, Karrie. Why don't you grow up?" Andrew looked out the window on his side of the car.

"Rainbows," said the policeman, over-enunciating each word in a childish voice as if he were talking to kindergartners, "happen when water from raindrops slow down the rays of light from the sun, and rainbows shows us all the properties of light."

"A rainbow," Andrew coldly said, looking at the policeman, "is caused by both reflection and refraction of light in water drops, which causes a spectrum of light to appear in the sky in the form of a bow."

The policewoman started to laugh.

"So you like science, huh, Andrew?" She turned around and smiled at him.

"I don't like being here," Andrew said, and he turned to look out the window again.

Karrie explained, "Pastor Will said that a rainbow is a promise from God."

Andrew turned and looked back at Karrie. "Really, Karrie, you're still talking religion? So, what promise did Pastor Will say God made with a rainbow?"

"That God wouldn't destroy everything. He always leaves us something," Karrie said.

"But things still get destroyed, Karrie, it happens all the time," said Andrew. "But not everything gets destroyed—not everything in the whole world."

Karrie's voice was quivering; she was about to cry, and she didn't know why. Why was Andrew angry about rainbows? Why had he stopped loving her?

"Maybe let's just stop talking until we get to station," the policewoman said.

Chapter 9

When they arrived at the police station, the policeman and the policewoman got out of the car and walked Andrew and Karrie to a room with white plastic chairs lining pale green walls. A woman behind a plastic window motioned for the police officers to come over to the desk. Karrie sat down on one of the hard plastic chairs, but Andrew just stood and kept looking out the large glass doors.

The policeman turned around and said, "Okay, Andrew, let me walk you to the top of the stairs. There's somebody who wants to talk to you."

The policewoman sat by Karrie, who saw a grandmotherly-looking woman coming down the hall toward her carrying a teddy bear in her arms. She shook her head to let the lady know she didn't want the bear, but the lady placed it on the seat next to her anyway. She was too old for teddy bears. Didn't that lady know she was eleven years old?

"Nice bear," said the policewoman.

"Sure, if you're a baby," said Karrie.

The lady at the desk motioned again to the policewoman. Karrie picked up the bear and ran her fingers through the white fur as soon as the policewoman had turned her back. Then the woman behind the desk called out Karrie's name. "Just go upstairs to the first door on the left," the woman said without looking up from her computer. "Doctor Ann will be talking to you today."

"Wait a minute," said the policewoman. "I need to come with you. Do you want me to carry the bear?"

"No," said Karrie. Her whole body felt numb as she got up from the chair and pulled the bear behind her as she slowly walked up the stairs. Karrie's back and head still hurt from her brother's kick. She was tired of crying, and she wanted to go home so bad it hurt. When she opened the door, she thought she was in the wrong place.

"This room is for babies," Karrie said.

Doctor Ann's office was painted blue and yellow with cartoon clouds scattered across the ceiling. There was a twisted rainbow on one side of the room that had bears and fairies sliding down its endless curve. In one corner, there was a table with Play-Doh and crayons on it.

On the other side of the room, there was a yellow couch with teen magazines scattered across the coffee table in front of it. The room was filled with games and toys of all sorts, yet to Karrie, it looked like a pre-school room. She slumped on the yellow couch next to the door. Doctor Ann smiled at her, and then they started to talk.

When Doctor Ann began her conversation with Karrie, it seemed as though they were talking about nothing. What were her favorite television shows? Who were her friends at school? What did she like to eat? What did she like about her church? What did she like to do when she got home from school?

And then, suddenly, they were talking about something. The fights between her mother and her father, Pete's nightmares and what came after Dad had beaten him up. As she described her father's visits, she began to sob again.

In the middle of the conversation, Karrie picked up the bear she had put on the floor and buried her face in its soft white fur. She talked about her father's visits to her room late at night, and she began to sob again.

"Why is Andrew mad at me?" Karrie asked after she wiped her tears on the white bear.

"Maybe, he's not angry at you. Maybe he's just angry," said Doctor Ann.

"No, he's angry at me! I can tell, and he never gets angry at anyone!" Karrie looked out the window. It had started to rain again. "He's angry because I told."

Doctor Ann gave Karrie a puzzled look. "Were you the one who told, Karrie? I want you think about that question before you answer it. Whom did you tell, Karrie? I know you just told me, but before this, who else did you tell?"

"Well, after I talked to Miss Dawn, the police came."

"The police came because your bother Pete kicked you in front of the church, and someone had called them," Doctor Ann corrected her.

"No one would call the police from our church," said Karrie, "because they knew it would get Pete into trouble, and Pastor Will and everyone else loves Pete. I remember Pastor Will praying for Pete. No, Pastor Will would not call the police."

"Karrie," Doctor Ann said firmly. "I don't know who called the police, but I agree with you. I don't think anyone at your church wanted to hurt Pete, but they knew something was wrong, and when mature adults know that children are in danger, they act in responsible ways to protect them from danger. Do you understand what I am saying, Karrie?"

"I don't think Pastor Will called the police." Karrie looked at Doctor Ann as hard as she could to make her point.

Somebody knocked at the door, and Doctor Ann looked at the clock on her desk. She opened an appointment book and began to write in it. "I am going to see you in a week, and then someone else will be seeing you," Doctor Ann said.

"Someone else?" asked Karrie. "Do I have to keep talking about this?"

"You don't have to talk about this subject when you are here, Karrie, if you don't want to. However, you will have to talk about this to the police and to the people in juvenile court and to a doctor who will examine you. But with me, you can talk about whatever you want to. I'm here to help you get through that experience."

"Can I go home now?"

"Not right away," Doctor Ann said. "You're going to have to see a physician tomorrow, and the police have to investigate the things you and Pete have said."

"Did Pete say the same things that I said?"

"I can't tell you what Pete said, but I can tell you no one thinks you are lying, Karrie—even Andrew." Doctor Ann got up to open the office door. "You said that you get along with your grandmother . . . They usually try to place children with their relatives. So maybe they will let you live with her for a little while."

The same lady that had handed Karrie the teddy bear was outside the door; this time she had a jelly doughnut in her hand.

"Why do people keep giving me things around here?" Karrie smiled at Doctor Ann, who shrugged her shoulders and turned up her hands and smiled back at her.

The grandmotherly woman walked Karrie out to the police car. The same policewoman that had driven her to the station was holding open the car's back seat door. Karrie scooted into the back seat, and the policewoman started the car.

"I see you got the bear and a doughnut," said the policewoman.

"Yeah," Karrie said. "They thought I was three years old, for some reason. Where's Andrew? Where are we going?"

"Tonight, Andrew is going to a group home for boys, and you are going to a group home for girls. Tomorrow, we'll pick up your things from your house."

"Don't I get to live with Andrew anymore?" Karrie asked.

"I'm sorry, honey. They don't tell us those things. I just know where I'm supposed to take you tonight." The policewoman smiled at Karrie through the rearview mirror. "Look, Karrie, there's another rainbow," she said as she turned the car around to get on the freeway ramp.

"This time there are two of them—one on top, and the other is inside the first one," Karrie said.

The police car sped up as it entered the freeway. Karrie's eyes didn't leave the rainbow. "Hey, it's following us! That's kind of . . . " Karrie couldn't think of the word she wanted to say.

"Magical?" the policewoman asked.

"No," Karrie said, "it is powerful."

Chapter 10

The policewoman had driven Karrie to house in a suburban neighborhood that Karrie had never seen before. There were rows and rows of houses that looked like those she had seen on reruns of *The Brady Bunch*. A slender black woman, whom the policewoman introduced as Miss Sophia, answered the door. Miss Sophia was a in her early twenties. She had long dreadlocks that fell down her back and were tied loosely together by a reggae scarf. The police officer introduced Karrie.

Miss Sophia smiled. "Pleased to meet you. Let me show you your room."

Karrie followed Miss Sophia through a large living that led into a hallway, and then she stopped at the second door and tapped lightly on the door.

"Yeah, come-in," the voice behind the door said.

A girl Karrie's age was stretched out on a bed underneath the window in the back of the room, checking her e-mail on her cell phone. She sat up when she saw Karrie enter the room.

"Lo'laini, this is Karrie," Miss Sophia said to the girl as she led Karrie into the room. Then she said to Karrie, "There's your bed, and your dresser is right beside it." Miss Sophia handed Karrie a small gift bag and then said to Lo'laini, "Help her get settled. Tomorrow morning, before breakfast we'll talk about the rules of the house. You got any questions?" Miss Sophia asked in a soft, motherly voice.

Karrie shrugged her shoulders.

"I'm just outside if you need me." Miss Sophia left the room.

Karrie stood there, looking at Lo'laini. She wasn't sure what to do next.

Lo'laini started to talk. "Okay, that side of the room is yours, and I'll leave it alone. But this side is mine, and you leave it alone." Lo'laini twisted her frizzy auburn hair and piled it on top of her head and stuck an orange rose clip in its crown, which held the disorderly bun tenuously together. "If you want to be a slob, you can be a slob. I don't care. My last roommate was a slob. I didn't tell on her, and I won't tell on you. I figured that was her business, not mine, but keep the mess on your side of the room and stay away from my stuff, okay?"

"Okay," Karrie said in a timid voice. Everything about Lo'laini was a surprise to Karrie. She had olive skin and high cheekbones and dark oval-shaped eyes. She had a tall, towering body and muscular arms, and her French-manicured nails were longer than any nails Karrie had ever seen on anyone's hands, except on people on television. She didn't have straight black hair like the Hawaiian girls Karrie had seen in magazines. Lo'laini had unruly auburn hair with a fiery red spark that showed in the sunlight. She seemed to speak with a British accent.

"I'm not going to be staying here for very long," Karrie said as she sat down on the bed on her side of the room. "I'm going to be moving in with Grandma."

"Is that what they told you?" Lo'laini's face softened as she studied Karrie's face, and she smiled at her and sat down on her bed.

Karrie had never had a best friend before. In fact, she had learned to maneuver her world alone from a young age. But there was something about Lo'laini that felt familiar. Karrie felt an innate kindness in her smile and Lo'laini's toughness didn't bother her. She knew after she sat on her bed she had made a friend for life.

"I'll tell you the truth," Lo'laini said. "Wait a week before you believe anything anyone has to tell you around here. They say lots of things to you at first because they feel sad about the stuff that happened to you. So they give you everything and tell you things you want hear. It's like when you try to stop a baby from crying by waving things in front of it that will make it laugh.

Just remember, just like with that baby, it's all just a game with them. They're trying to make things better when they know they really can't. It's your first time in foster care, huh?"

"Yeah." Karrie picked up the bear that was given to her at the police station and buried her face into its soft white fur. "I miss my mom, my grandma, and Andrew," Karrie mumbled in the fur.

"Is Andrew your boyfriend?" asked Lo'laini.

"No," laughed Karrie. "I don't have a boyfriend. I'm too young. Andrew is my brother. He's my favorite brother, and now he hates me. I know he does because of all of this."

"Maybe not," said Lo'laini. "Even if he does hate you, hate doesn't last forever. Sometimes it just lasts until you stop being angry." Lo'laini reached up to the top of her dresser and pulled down a silver picture frame. "That's my boyfriend. His name is Kevin." Lo'laini handed Karrie the picture of a tall, gangly teenage boy with dark brown hair that framed his face. He was standing beside a surfboard.

"Wow," said Karrie, "he's cute!"

"You better believe it, and he's all mine, so don't get any ideas." Lo'laini took the picture back and cradled it in her arms. "When this is all over and I'm eighteen, we're going to get married and move back to the Islands."

"So you are from Hawaii?" asked Karrie.

"Yeah, I loved it there. I hated it when my dad said we had to move." Lo'laini lay back on her bed while looking at her boyfriend's picture.

"Why'd you have to move?" asked Karrie.

"My mom got sick," Lo'laini said. "Funny, I don't remember her being very sick for long, so I guess she kept it a secret for a long while. Then she died, and my dad said we had to move."

"How did she die?" asked Karrie.

"She didn't die all at once. She died, but bit by bit."

"How does someone die bit by bit?" asked Karrie.

"Cancer. Every day I think about her telling me. She came home from the doctor and said she wanted to take a walk with me on the beach. There was this lagoon that none of the tourists ever visited that she used to take me to when I was a little girl. I loved that place. It had this little playground, and we'd both dig in the sand. The top sand was white. Underneath, it was golden, and deep down it was dark. I'd always tell my mom we could dig far enough to reach China if we'd just stay there all day."

Lo'laini put the silver picture frame back on her dresser. She crossed her arms over her head to make a pillow for her head with her hands and she stretched out her long body over the bed. Looking at the ceiling she kept talking. "But we didn't dig in the sand that day. We both sat down on the edge of the sandbox, and then she started to talk about God and Jesus and heaven, and then she hugged me so tight I couldn't breathe. I didn't know what to say. I understood she was saying something serious, but I really didn't understand. After that day, we started to go to church, like every night. We all went to this church where my mom and my dad met. Dad came to the Islands after he came back from fighting in Afghanistan. He was having nightmares, and he said the islands quieted them. He met Mom at church, and they got married there. That church was our wholes lives. Everyone knew us there, and we knew everyone. Everyone would pray and cry and put oil on her head. Everyone was praying and saying she was going to get better, but then she didn't. She told me once she knew she wasn't going to get better. She wanted me to know she would be okay, if she went to heaven. The only thing was that Dad and I weren't okay."

Lo'laini brushed aside a round tear that fell down the side of her cheek. "Boy, I'm talking to you more than anyone else I've met. What's up with that?"

Karrie just shrugged her shoulders. "Anyway, I went on this church retreat with the youth group and we were hiking up this mountain. I felt so alone there, and I knew everyone was watching me because of what was happening to my mom, but no one would talk to me. I didn't know what to do.

Should I act like a good Christian and talk about heaven or should scream or yell. I couldn't do any of those things, so I started to sing this song I learned in preschool under my breath."

"You sang a song you learned in preschool under breath?" Karrie looked over at Lo'laini who now had eyes closed.

"Yeah, I used to cry when mom would drop me off there in morning and teacher would sing this song to the tune reveille." Lo'laini started sing in a hushed tone. "Mommy will come back, mommy will come back, Mommy will come back to get you, Mommy will never forget." Lo'laini's voice tapered out again, big tears fell down the side of her face.

"So Kevin heard me sing the song on hike and by the camp fire he started to play it quietly on his guitar. At first I thought he was teasing me then I looked up at his face and I saw he wasn't. We talked for four hours that night. He lived close by and I'd go to his house when Dad got mad because Mom was sick. I remember the last time Mom went into the hospital and I realized that she wasn't living any more, she was dying. I didn't want to ride in the car with my dad, because he was angry all the time, so I took the bus and went to Kevin's house. I sat and cried for a long time. We both cried actually. Then we both started to sing. 'Mommy will come back, Mommy will come back, Mommy will come back to get you, Mommy will never forget.'"

Lo'laini sat up again and looked directly at Karrie, "So you see that's why I got to marry Kevin, that's why it can't be anyone else, he's the only one who ever understood. He's the only one who could ever understand."

Karrie nodded back.

"So anyway, when Mom died, or should I say when my mom finished dying, Dad changed. He got angry and mean. Dad didn't even want to go to Mom's funeral. 'Not in that church!' he screamed at my grandma one day. He said he hated those islands and the superstitions of the church. He said they were the reason my mom was sick. It didn't make any sense to me because Mom was born there, and we had lived there all our lives. Dad used to say those islands had changed his life. He said the same thing about the church, and now he hated them both and everyone in them. Grandma just sat there like a stone, shaking her head when he started to scream at her. She said, 'I know this isn't you talking right now. I know you, and this is not the way you feel. Something else is talking—something unreal and untrue, and I won't hear it.' I was proud of my grandma sitting there calmly while he screamed and not answering back the same way. But I still think it was a mean thing for him to say to my grandma, and I knew he wanted to hurt her, and it made me angry."

Lo'laini sighed, and then she laid down again. "So we had to move to California. I think he wanted to hurt my grandma, but Kevin and I kept e-mailing, messaging, texting, and calling, so I still think he's my boyfriend."

"But how did you get here? Did your dad hurt you?" asked Karrie.

"No." Lo'laini' sighed and rolled her eyes. "He hurt himself. When we were in California, he started to hang around his old military buddies, and they started talking about the war, getting drunk and smoking weed, and then doing some other drugs. He was stoned all the time. It was like he was a different person. I think he must've been dealing the stuff. Anyway, one day I came home from school, and all his friends and him were stoned in the living room, and the police were searching the place. They went in the kitchen and pulled all pots and pans out of the cupboards and threw them on the floor. Then they poured out the flour and sugar all over the floor. Then they went out onto the back porch, and they dumped all my mom's stuff out of her chest onto the back porch floor. It was all I had left of her, and they were throwing it around like it was garbage! I hated seeing all her private stuff lying out there in the open like that."

Lo'laini looked up at the ceiling for a while. She had stopped talking, and Karrie wasn't sure if she was finished. Then she said in a trembling voice, "They took Dad away, and I came here. I wanted to go to my grandma's, too. The lawyer said I might go there, but they haven't sent me yet. I don't think they ever will send me, even though at first they said they might. So I'm just warning you, don't believe everything they tell you here."

Karrie lay down on her bed. She looked around at the yellow-greenish walls and the plain, drab curtains. The room reminded her more of a hotel room than a teenage girl's bedroom. There was nothing really personal about the room. No posters or stickers someone would usually see in a teenager's room. Lo'laini had her stuff neatly put away. The only thing she had out was the picture of Kevin. She seemed to be keeping herself ready to leave at a moment's notice if she needed to leave.

The room seemed soulless, as if it was resisting being defined as a home and reminding its occupants their stay there was temporary. Then Karrie looked at the brown nightstand by her bed, and her heart leaped when she saw her Bible. She grabbed it and held it close to her chest. "My Bible!" she said.

"Yeah," Lo'laini said, wiping her face and sitting up in her bed. "The policewoman brought it here this afternoon before you came here. She said you left it in the car when they first picked you up at the church. So you're a Christian, too, I guess."

"Yeah," said Karrie, thumbing through the old folded pages. "So, do you still believe in God and Jesus? I mean, after everything that happened—when your mom didn't get better and then your dad acted the way he did."

"Yeah, I believe in God and Jesus," said Lo'laini. "I just don't believe much in my dad. What he did was stupid, and it messed everything up. I don't believe that the prayers at church didn't work like my dad said. I saw my mom's face when they said those prayers, and something was happening in her because they prayed. I still go to church. There's one on the corner—we can walk there on Sunday morning, if you want." Then Lo'laini leaned in and started to whisper, "I've got to tell you, though: it's hard to be Christian around here. Everyone cusses, lies, steals—even the grownups. You're going to have to lock all your stuff up, and you can't turn the other cheek around here. You really got to take care of yourself, or things can go bad for you." Lo'laini stopped talking and looked at her nails in the lamplight next to her bed. Each one glistened a pink hue. "With Mom gone, sometimes I feel like I have forgotten how to act like a Christian. I still sometimes feel like I can feel God looking after me, but I don't tell people in this place. It would just cause a fight. You don't want to be picked on in this place. Trust me on that one." They both sat quiet for a moment. Karrie was looking at the carpet floor, and Lo'laini was looking at Karrie. "I'm sorry," Lo'laini said.

"Sorry for what?" Karrie said while still looking at the floor.

"For everything. I'm sorry for the whole stinky world." Lo'laini lay back on her bed again.

"Girls, lights out in twenty minutes!" said Miss Sophia as she entered the room carrying a book in her hand. She turned out the lights and then went back into the living room and curled up on the couch.

"She always has a book in her hand," whispered Lo'laini after Miss Sophia left the room. "She's the coolest of all the house parents here!"

"Yeah," said Karrie, "She looks our age!"

"No, "whispered Lo'laini, "She's just short, she's in her early twenties I figure. Some of the girls think she has a rich boyfriend who may be a rock star."

"Why do they think that?" asked Karrie.

"Because she has a guitar she brings to work sometimes and some of the girls can hear her strum it in the late hours of the night after she thinks everyone is asleep."

Karrie then noticed Miss Sophia at the door and put a finger to her lips signaling Lo'laini to stop talking. They both watched Miss Sophia as she smiled and said loud enough so they could hear, "You're correct on one point only. I *am* a twenty-year-old college student. Now get ready to go to bed, it is going to be a busy day tomorrow."

Miss Sophia closed the door halfway and returned again to the living room couch.

Karrie watched through the crack of the door as Miss Sophia opened her computer and saw the screensaver of her and her boyfriend De'Angre standing on the pier of Pacific Beach. Miss Sophia whispered to herself while looking at the skinny service man laughing beside her, It would be nice to have a rich boyfriend, but I guess you'll do me just fine. I wish you were living here," she said to the silent image on the screen before her. "I'd come home to you after work and school, instead of my parents."

Miss Sophia looked up into the silence of the night and whispered, "Stop daydreaming girl, you have to study tonight. There are times I think I am just making you up, you've been gone for so long. I hope that Navy-paid education is worth all this." She kissed her fingers and touched the computer screen.

Suddenly, Lo'laini laughed at Karrie and interrupted her observation of Miss Sophia. "You got to stop spying on Miss Sophia and get ready for bed."

"What am I going to wear to bed?" Karrie suddenly realized she hadn't brought anything with her.

"The gift bag that I gave you when you came in is a welcome kit. It has everything you'll need for tonight until they get your stuff from your house tomorrow," said Lo'laini.

"Lo'laini, are you making Karrie feel welcome?" shouted Miss Sophia from the living room.

"I'm the most welcoming person in the whole world," Lo'laini said. Then she looked at Karrie. "One of the house parents will take you shopping in the next few days to get you some new stuff."

Karrie started to open the brown box. It had several pairs of new underwear, a nightshirt, and some feminine products.

"So what did you get?" Lo'laini asked as she sat up on the side of her bed. "A Padres nightshirt or a Dodger one?"

"Padres," Karrie said as she held up the striped baseball nightshirt against her chest. "I don't think I'll need this yet," Karrie said as she held up a bra.

"Yes, I think you do. In fact, someone should have bought you one before now," Lo'laini started to laugh.

Karrie quickly folded her arms across her chest.

Karrie stepped in the closet for some privacy and slipped off her shirt and jeans and slipped on her new night shirt. The lights were out when she walked out of the closet. She climbed into bed and pulled the covers over her. The sheets crackled when she turned on her side.

"Don't mind that," Lo'laini said. "They cover all the beds here in plastic sheets in case someone pees their bed."

Karrie's sheets smelled like lilac and a soft, yet firm pillow held her head at the perfect angle. Karrie missed her mom and her brother, but it felt so good to be in between two warm freshly washed sheets in a house that didn't smell like yesterday's garbage, and to know that her father couldn't visit her that night. She felt herself sinking into a deep sleep.

"So do you still believe in God after everything that has happened to you?" asked Lo'laini.

"How do you know what happened to me? I haven't told you anything yet." Karrie yawned with her half-opened eyes weighed down with the desire to sleep.

"I can see it. It's in your eyes, and I've seen it before," Lo'laini said, "Girls have sad eyes after certain things happen to them."

There was a long moment of silence. Karrie could hear a girl in the next room sobbing. "Yeah," she whispered. "I still believe. I don't put the two things together. I mean, I don't think God had anything to do with the things that happened to me at home." She wiggled her body deeper between the sheets. "Church was so different from home. I never really could connect the things that were said at church to the things that happened in my house. Two different worlds, I guess." She yawned again. Her words started to blend together, blurring with her fatigue. "I still believe because, like you said, sometimes I can feel God, like in the wind and rainbows."

"Rainbows?" Lo'laini laughed. "Girl, you must be trippin'. That's not something in the Bible. It sounds like Care Bears or something."

"No, not like Care Bears, like Noah." Karrie yawned again. "Pastor Will said a rainbow was a promise from God." Her last phrase was swallowed up in a final giant yawn; her body was melting into sleep.

With her eyes closed, she could see the twisted rainbow in the therapist's office with bears and fairies sliding perpetually down its curves. Then beyond the rainbow, she saw her church's patio and Pastor Will calling out her name. He was looking frantically for her, but she was standing there on the patio the whole time. Why couldn't he see her? She opened her mouth to call out to Pastor Will, but her tongue was heavy and fat and filled up her mouth so she couldn't cry out to him. Then her throbbing body began to relax and sink into the lilac scented sheets, and she was asleep.

Chapter 11

When Karrie woke up, all the other girls in the house were gone. A large, middle-aged woman with a kind smile greeted her. "I thought you might like to sleep in, after everything that happened yesterday."

Karrie stretched and nodded and smiled.

"My name is Miss Ellen," said the kind-faced woman standing in the door. "After you shower, there are pancakes in the dining room."

"I have to shower?" asked Karrie.

"We shower every day here, Karrie," Miss Ellen said holding up a clipboard so Karrie could see the printed schedule with boxes highlighted by yellow, pink, and blue markers. "During breakfast, I'll go over today's schedule with you."

"There's a schedule?"

"I know, there's so much for you to learn," Miss Ellen said over her shoulder as she went back into the kitchen. Karrie got up and showered. She put on the same wrinkled jeans and top she'd had on the day before.

While Karrie ate, Miss Ellen went over the list of appointments she had for the day. She would visit another doctor for a second examination. Miss Ellen said she would also drive Karrie back to her house to pick up some things.

"Will Mom be there?" Karrie sheepishly looked up at Miss Ellen.

Miss Ellen shook her head. "You might be able to see her later on today if you would like to."

"I would."

Then Miss Ellen told her there were judges, social workers, and lawyers that wanted to see her. Then tomorrow they would register her at her new school. Karrie sat quietly in the station wagon as Miss Ellen drove her to the doctor's office. He asked all the same questions the doctor had asked at the police station the night before.

When Karrie asked Miss Ellen why she had to have two examinations, Miss Ellen quietly said, "Each doctor was looking for different things." Then she drove Karrie to back to her old home.

When Miss Ellen opened the front door and saw her family's trash scattered across the living room, Karrie's face flushed red; but Miss Ellen simply stepped over the trash as if it were commonplace. They walked to the back of the house to Karrie's room, where Karrie emptied out her dresser drawers of clothing into plastic trash bags.

Next, they drove to the courthouse, where the judge read Karrie's interview from Doctor Ann's report and asked Karrie about the group home and how she was feeling.

Karrie felt numb and confused, and her body ached all over. She simply nodded at him and said, "Good," when he asked.

Then Karrie and Ellen were back at the police station in the cold, uncomfortable white plastic chairs. Miss Ellen took out a bag of yarn and a crochet hook and began to work. Karrie looked up at Miss Ellen, examining her wrinkled kind face.

"Lo'laini says all the girls at the group home call you the farmer's wife," said Karrie as she swung her legs back and forth under the white plastic chair in the children's court waiting room.

"So they call me a farmer's wife?" Ellen chuckled to herself.

"Yeah, that's what Lo'laini says they call you."

"Do they, indeed," said Miss Ellen as her nibbled fingers continued to work gracefully, pulling a crochet hook through small loops of colorful yarn. She put down her needlework for a moment, and her big, pale-blue eyes looked at Karrie over her pink-rimmed reading glasses. "Well, I guess that fits me fine."

Karrie thought Miss Ellen's body was shaped like one of the Kewpie dolls that were at the Del Mar fair game booths she had seen each year. Miss Ellen's head was surrounded by golden-gray curls. She had apple cheeks and a dimple in her chin. She had round, soft arms—they were the kind of arms that beg children to squeeze and snuggle their noses in the rolls of soft fat to find comfort. Karrie was much too big to indulge in such a practice, so she rested her head against the pillowed arms instead. "Is your husband a farmer?" she asked.

"No," said Miss Ellen. "He's an English teacher, and I am a retired English teacher."

"Is Miss Sophia's boyfriend really a rock star?"

"No." Miss Ellen smiled. "But I think you should tell her that so she could have a laugh."

Miss Ellen turned her head to look at the policewoman who was suddenly standing in front of them. "How can we help you?"

The policewoman sat down next to Karrie. "We've got one more interview, Karrie—that is, if you are up to it."

"My dad?" asked Karrie.

"No," said the policewoman, "your mom wants to speak to you."

At the mention of the words "your mom," Karrie felt a thrill of excitement. Then she felt a pain in her chest. She knew Mama would be angry and hurt, but she wanted to see her anyway. She looked up at Miss Ellen, hoping she would nod yes or no as to whether she should see her mom. However, Miss Ellen looked pleasantly back at her and did not nod her head one way or another.

"Yes, I want to see my mom. Will you wait?" she asked Miss Ellen.

"Of course," said Ellen as she resumed her crochet work.

The policewoman walked Karrie down the long, light green hallway lined on each side with long wooden rectangle doors. Each door had a small window at the top of it darkened by crisscrossed wires. They stopped when they reached the last door on the left. The policewoman pulled out a ring of keys and opened the heavy wooden door. The room wasn't much bigger than a large closet. It had just enough room to hold a small table with four chairs around it. Mama was sitting there, shaking; her face and chest were red. She was violently wringing her hands as if she was trying to scrape something off them. She was rubbing her hands so harshly Karrie was frightened she was going to tear the skin off her palms.

Karrie ran around to the other side of the table to her mother. They both hugged and then sat down. The policewoman leaned against the back wall. "So I guess you've got to stay here, huh?" Mama said, looking up at the policewoman.

"Yes, ma'am, I do," she replied.

"So, are you being good? Are you behaving yourself?" Mama asked Karrie while tightly squeezing her hand.

"Yes, Mama, I am."

"And you're not causing anyone any trouble, are you?" Mama asked.

Karrie shook her head to say no.

"So I guess we got ourselves into a lot a trouble here." Mama looked directly at her daughter.

There was a long moment of silence. Karrie knew she was supposed to say something, but she wasn't sure what it should be. Mama stared at her so intensely that Karrie had to break the silence, and so she said the first thing that came to her mind.

"Mama, I saw a double rainbow yesterday!"

"Is that all you've got to say to me, little girl?" Mama hissed from across the table.

"Ma'am, I need you to calm down and use a civil voice with your daughter," the officer said as she moved closer to the table.

Mama lifted her hands as if she was giving up in a fight, and the policewoman retreated to stand against the wall.

"I just don't know what do with you sometimes, child. You sometimes talk like a grown-up preacher, and no one understands what you're saying. People don't like it, Karrie, they really don't. Then something pops out of your mouth like that 'I saw a rainbow,' and you sound like a baby. How old are you, three? Your head's always in the clouds, girl."

Mama looked up at the policewoman to make sure that her voice wasn't too loud.

Then she whispered to her daughter, "You better be right, Karrie. You better be right in what you're saying about your dad. A lot of things have gotten broken here that can't be fixed. Now you look fine, but your brother, Andrew? Well, I just saw him this morning, and things aren't going as good for him. Seems he's got a black eye. Someone beat him up."

Karrie gasped.

"Ma'am," the policewoman said in a warning tone.

"And we might lose the house. Is that what you want?"

"No, Mama," Karrie said.

"Ma'am, you understood what the judge said when he said you may not threaten your daughter." The policewoman now sat down at the table.

"And do you understand what I'm telling you when I say don't threaten me, lady?" Mama stood up from the table. "I love my kids, just as much as you love yours." Karrie's mother backed up against the wall as if she were a trapped animal. She covered her face with her hands and took a deep breath and wiped her face. "You know, lady, I saw this television show the other day. It was a show about the famine in Somalia, and there was this mother who was trying to nurse her baby, but no milk was coming out. It wasn't that she didn't love her baby—it was just that she didn't have any milk 'cause she was starving, too. So both Mama and baby cried. They cried because there was no milk. It wasn't right, it wasn't fair, it just *was*."

Mama's voice was rising throughout her speech, and now she was screaming. "Now you're going to take my babies away! You're going to take them away so I can't even try to nurse them!" Mama started to cry.

"No, Mama," Karrie cried out. "I'm not going to go far away. I'm just going to go live with Grandma so you can visit us all the time."

"Karrie, you can't go live with your grandma," Mama shouted at her, "because your grandma's old and sick, and she's going to have to sell the house so she can go to assisted living."

"But what about her garden?" Karrie said, looking down at her hands.

"Yeah, her garden. That's what you're worried about, little girl?"

"What about Aunt Mary?" asked Karrie.

"Well, she lives in Arizona, doesn't she?" Mama said. "Now, I guess you can go there, but if you do, I'm never going to get to see ya."

"I guess I didn't figure on that," said Karrie.

"Well, there's a lot you don't know, because you are a kid, even though you don't act like it sometimes. But you are still a kid! So you should be careful next time you go blabbing your mouth off to strangers!" Then Mama lunged at her.

The policewoman blocked her and pushed her back into the chair behind her. "I am sorry, this interview has just ended," said the policewoman. Then with her hands firmly on Karrie's shoulders, she pushed Karrie out of the room into the hall.

Karrie could hear her mother crying in the small room behind her, and the policewoman firmly walked her down the hall. Miss Ellen stood up when she saw Karrie walking down the hall and began to walk toward her. Karrie ran into her arms, and in a moment of mercy, her warm, flushed, reddened face rested in Miss Ellen's cool, soft arms, and she began to cry.

"I broke my family. I broke my family."

Chapter 12

By the time Karrie and Miss Ellen reached the group home, the house was dark, and all the girls were asleep. When Karrie walked in the front door, she saw Miss Sophia sitting at the dining room table. She was writing under a small lamp that illuminated sheets of white paper that were scattered across the table. Miss Sophia had a pencil in one hand and a Diet Pepsi in the other with her computer open on one side of her and her calculator on the other side.

"So you two are finally back," she said as they entered the living room. She stood up, stretching her arms and yawning. "We saved some spaghetti for you, Karrie. Are you hungry?"

"Karrie already told me she wasn't hungry, but I think some ice cream would do the trick," said Miss Ellen. "Can I talk to you for a moment, Miss Sophia?"

"Sure." Miss Sophia got up from the table and went into the kitchen and came back to Karrie with a blue bowl of Neapolitan ice cream with a spoon stuck on top of it like a flag. "Now this is my favorite place to sit at night," she said, clearing off a corner of the table, "because you can see the moon from here, right outside that window."

Then Miss Sophia and Miss Ellen walked to the office at the end of the hall and closed the door. Karrie stirred her ice cream in the dish until all the colors blended together into a light reddish brown. She examined the papers on the table. Some had long rows of numbers separated by addition, subtraction, some in parentheses. Other papers had a list of numbered sentences and paragraphs. On the screensaver on Miss Sophia's laptop, there was picture of a sailor leaning off the pier at the beach. He had his mouth open and was waving his arms as if he was pretending he was falling off the edge. Miss Sophia was holding him by his tie as if she were pulling him back from falling while she was calmly leaning against a lamppost. She was smiling as she stared straight at the camera. When Karrie heard the office door creak open, she looked back at her ice cream.

"Good night, Karrie," said Miss Ellen as she walked across the room. "I'll see ya tomorrow."

"Good night, Miss Ellen," said Karrie.

Miss Sophia came back to the table and started to gather the scattered papers. "Ellen said you had a rough day today, Karrie," she said as she stacked her papers into three neat little piles. "Do you want to talk about it?"

"No," said Karrie as she picked up one of the papers that had fallen under the table. "Is this algebra?"

"Yes," replied Miss Sophia as she took the sheet of paper from Karrie and put it on one of her piles.

"Is algebra the kind of math where you turn word problems into numbers problems to get the answers?"

"Algebra is one of the kinds of math where you turn word problems into mathematical equations, but there are other kinds of math that do that as well."

"Do you like it?" asked Karrie.

"Yes, I do," said Miss Sophia as she put her piles of paper into her computer case. "My dad taught it to me when I was in elementary school. He is an engineer and the smartest man I know. He loves math, so I guess it was the way he talked about it that made me love it as well."

"Do you think all problems can be turned into numbers to make equations?" asked Karrie.

"No, honey. Not all problems can be solved by mathematical equations." Miss Sophia examined Karrie's face. Karrie didn't say a word.

Miss Sophia picked up her papers and put them into folders and shoved them into a backpack. Then she smiled and said, "Although, my grandpa might disagree with me on that last point."

"Is your grandpa an engineer, too?" asked Karrie.

"No, he is a preacher."

"So you go to church?"

"Yes, I do, when I've got a day off. You know, that ice cream looks really good. If you don't mind, I'm going to go get myself a bowl of it." Miss Sophia left a moment, and Karrie found another piece of paper that had fallen under the table. She examined the long rows of numbers on the papers on the table.

"So do you live with your grandpa?" asked Karrie when Miss Sophia came back into the room.

"No, I still live with my mom and my dad while I'm working through school."

"Do your dad and your Grandpa fight about it?"

"Fight about what?" Miss Sophia asked.

"About the numbers—do they fight about numbers, solving all problems?"

"Now I wouldn't call it a fight—just a powerful disagreement. My dad and Grandpa have this ongoing argument where Grandpa says all solutions lead to God, and Dad says that Grandpa is twisting the numbers or data to make them mean what he wants them to mean. Sometimes in church, when Grandpa tries to prove God's existence through numbers or science, my dad will start to mumble and whisper to my mom, 'What is that old man doing?' My mom jabs my dad in the side to get him to be quiet.

"Then during Sunday afternoon lunch, those two will start arguing. It always ends up with Grandpa's billowing voice saying, 'All knowledge is God's knowledge.' My dad would shout back, 'You can't make something prove something just because you want it, too.'"

Miss Sophia started laughing while stirring her ice cream as she stared into her bowl. Then she looked up at the moon through the window above Karrie's head. "Wow, isn't that a lovely thing to gaze at this evening?"

"Does it make you scared when your grandpa and your dad fight?" asked Karrie.

"No, it's not that kind of fight. We don't have those kinds of fights in our home. I have to tell you, I didn't know people could be so unkind and cruel in their family fights until I took this job. Whenever I start to feel sorry for myself because I don't have a car or I work too much, I think of you girls and what you have to face. I think you're all pretty strong young women."

"I made my mom cry today," said Karrie.

"Karrie, you didn't make your mom do anything. She's a grown-up woman, and her tears have more to do with her than with you. Your family is just realizing they are broken, and they are blaming it on you. No teenager can break an entire family, and certainly, no teenager can hold up a grown woman or keep her from crying. No person can be held up if they don't want to stand up—not even by the strongest hands."

Karrie looked up at the moon. It had a light-blue glow around it, and the stars faded in the background behind it. "What holds up the moon?" she whispered to herself.

"Gravity," Miss Sophia whispered back. "Now, why that moon is held up— that's a question for religion."

"I thought you weren't supposed to talk about God," Karrie said, smiling up at Miss Sophia.

"I'm not talking about God. Did you hear me say God?" Miss Sophia winked at Karrie. "We're just having an educational, philosophical conversation."

"Ellen and Doctor Ann said the same thing about my mom that you did, but it doesn't seem true to me right now. I'm scared I hurt my mom in a way that I can't take back," Karrie said. "What happens to me if my family falls apart?"

"My guess is that your mama won't fall apart," said Miss Sophia. "She's stronger than she thinks. She's probably taken some tumbles before, and she'll take some tumbles again, but she'll find herself able to get up and stand again. We all do. The trick to finding out how strong a person is sometimes is to let the person fall so they figure out how to get up on their own. Anyway, you'll be fine. After all this, you may go back to living with your mom, or you may live with someone else, but you'll get through this, Karrie, and so will your mom without having to rely on you to hold her up. But you got to let her be the grown-up and you be the kid."

Karrie looked again at the screensaver. "Who's that?" she asked.

"That," said Miss Sophia as she closed her laptop, "is none of your business." Her face brightened, and then she said, "Oh, I almost forgot. Lo'laini says you're going to church with her in two weeks, and she bought you something to wear." Miss Sophia handed Karrie a small rectangular cardboard box covered with clear plastic paper. Through the plastic, Karrie could see ten silver and gold push-on acrylic nails.

She held them up to the moon. "So we'll shine like stars."

But Karrie didn't get to go to church with Lo'laini that Sunday. It would be three years before Karrie's mother would let her go to church.

"They'll turn you against me," Karrie's mother would tell her on her visitations. It took Karrie's mother another year before Karrie's mom would agree to see her. Their relationship was shaky at best and Karrie didn't want to jinx it.

The group home was difficult at first, but Karrie settled in. Lo'laini helped her keep her guard up and not let anyone get too close. Court dates, visits to therapist and case managers seemed to all blur into one exercise of smiling and talking politely about things she thought were no one's business. Karrie knew she wasn't supposed to defend her mother, but she didn't much care for professional people who were constantly questioning her. The worst interviews were the ones with potential foster parents. Karrie didn't want to move into a foster home. Somehow moving from the group home felt like she was betraying her mother. So she refused each home at her mother's request and simply told the other social workers she didn't want to talk to any more foster families.

Then while visiting on Karrie's fourteenth birthday, her mom unexpectedly asked her, "So are you still going to church? You used to love going to church. What's the matter with you?"

"You said you didn't want me to go to church. That they were going to poison me against you," Karrie stammered back.

"No, you must've dreamt that. Go back to church. You can go with your friend Lo'laini," Karrie's mother said as she lit another cigarette.

Karrie smiled at the small prayer request answered by her mother's reply.

Chapter 13

Lo'laini and Karrie spent two hours getting ready for church that morning. Lo'laini told Karrie they needed to make an entrance into the youth group Sunday morning. She wore a simple blue dress that fell loosely over her body with a skirt that slightly flared out at the bottom. She had bamboo flip flops on her feet with light-blue velvet straps. She had French-braided her hair into a long braid so the different highlights of her brown-and-red hair contrasted as it wove down her back.

Karrie had a new pink-and-white dress she had bought when she went shopping with Miss Ellen for her birthday. The pink fabric had colorful ribbons that wove in and out of each other across the dress. She wore white flat shoes with a little bow resting on top of the tip of her toes. Both girls had long gold-and-silver-tipped acrylic nails. Lo'laini helped Karrie with the curling iron that morning to make little curls that fell down her back.

Miss Ellen walked them the two blocks toward a church that took up a whole third block. To Karrie it looked more like a shopping center. Another lady from church stood at the end of the block; she was also a foster parent, and she would be in charge of them. When they reached the end of the block, Miss Ellen made the introductions.

"Karrie, this is Ms. Wright. She's going to be watching over you at church today," Miss Ellen started to say when Lo'laini interrupted.

"No, let me tell the rest. She's my friend," Lo'laini said as she stepped between Karrie and Miss Ellen.

"Not your friend, but your temporary guardian when you're at church," corrected Ms. Wright with a smile.

"Okay, guardian," conceded Lo'laini. "But she's really nice, Karrie, and her house has a pool! She'll walk us to the youth department, and then afterwards, we meet her at the information booth."

"Thank-you, Lo'laini, for filling Karrie in on all the details," said Miss Ellen. "Why don't you two girls go stand by the storefront behind us while Ms. Wright and I exchange paperwork and information."

Lo'laini rolled her eyes and pulled Karrie back toward a large window in front of the furniture store. "I hate it when grown-ups treat us as babies," she mumbled under her breath.

The furniture store had a large antique mirror in it that faced the street. Karrie could see her reflection in the mirror. She had never had such pretty clothes before. No way could her mother ever afford to buy her these kinds of clothes. Karrie couldn't get that thought out of her head when she was shopping with Miss Ellen on Saturday morning. Her mom's speech at the police department echoed through her head above the mall's background music. Her mother's warning about people turning Karrie against her was constantly buzzing in her ears. Her new dress fell over her body like it was perfectly cut for her to wear, but so did a heavy blanket of guilt accompanied by the echo of her mother's tears.

When Lo'laini caught Karrie looking down at the ground, she jabbed her in the side with her elbow. "No sad thoughts today, girl!" Lo'laini smiled from ear to ear. "We're out of that house today, and we are looking good. We will dazzle everyone when we walk in that room. I love this youth group. I'm not going to be sad while we're there, so don't make me sad. Don't bring that house into the youth group, okay?"

Karrie nodded. "I'm a little nervous with the nails." Karrie wiggled her fingers in the sun. "What if I have to open my Bible or scratch myself or something?"

"Scratch lightly. And use the flat part of your fingers to open anything."

"What if I have to pick my nose?" Karrie laughed.

"Gross!" Lo'laini squealed. "If you have to pick your nose, don't sit next to me!"

"Well, it's better than passing gas," laughed Karrie. "You let loose some big ones in your sleep last night, Lo'laini."

"It was those bean burritos Miss Sophia served last night. They tasted good going down, but they didn't smell too good coming out. Everyone in the house felt it. I swear that house was floating on a green cloud last night! So maybe we'll dazzle them with bodily functions." Lo'laini giggled.

"Okay, girls," said Ms. Wright, "transfer completed. So let's get across the street to church."

As they crossed the street, the church complex looked more intimidating to Karrie. The parking lot was full of shiny new cars, with smartly dressed families. Parents were smoothing out children's hair and smoothing the wrinkles in their clothing from the ride over to church. After cleaning off their children, the parents would swoop up babies onto their hips and grab young children by their hand and walk in a rapid pace toward the big red church doors, trying to get kids to Sunday school and to the nursery before church started.

Next to the church was a brown rectangular building—the youth center. In small clusters of three and four, junior high and high school kids stood out in front of the building, talking and laughing. Karrie looked up at Lo'laini for a moment, and she thought she saw her complexion white with fear. Then Ms. Wright waved at the one of the adults in the crowd, and the man waved back.

"That's Pastor Mike," Lo'laini whispered into Karrie's ear and then grabbed her arm, and they walked into the crowd of kids, with Ms. Wright following at a distance. By the time Karrie and Lo'laini reached the porch, Pastor Mike was herding the kids into the doors of the youth center.

"Hey, Lo'laini," said Pastor Mike, "who's your new friend?"

Pastor Mike didn't look like Pastor Will at all. Pastor Will always had a suit on. Karrie's father had once joked that Pastor Will probably showered with a suit and tie on. The youth leaders at Karrie's church didn't wear ties like Pastor Will, but they always wore church clothes, which were button-down shirts and slacks; but those rules didn't seem to apply here. Pastor Mike had on a pair of brown long shorts and a blue T-shirt that read "Kickin' it with Jesus" in bubble letters across the top. He had sandals on his feet, and his hair was wet.

"This is Karrie. She's visiting me for a little while," Lo'laini said while pushing Karrie forward.

Visiting her? What did she mean? Did Pastor Mike not know about the group home? Didn't he see Ms. Wright behind them? Why was Lo'laini pretending? Lying to the minister seemed like a horrible sin.

"Where are you visiting us from?" Pastor Mike asked Karrie.

"I'm from San Diego, too," said Karrie. "I live in Golden Hills on Thirtieth Street near Logan Heights."

"Well, welcome, Karrie," said Pastor Mike. "Come on in!"

Karrie and Lo'laini walked into the big auditorium filled with folding chairs. There was a band playing on the small stage in front of the auditorium—two guys on guitar and two girls with microphones. They were singing, "Welcome to this place! Come and fill this place! We are here to worship!"

Karrie and Lo'laini found two seats in the back of the room while the rest of the kids scurried around looking for seats where they could sit in the safety of their friends' protection.

Pastor Mike walked to the center of the room. "Okay, everyone, quiet down."

The giggles and shouts were quieted into whispers and nudges.

"Okay, we're dividing up into small groups, and I want about twelve groups of three to four kids in each group."

The kids started to get up and look around. "And I don't want you just sitting with your friends." Pastor Mike looked around the room while shaking his finger.

"Who do you want us to sit with? Our enemies?" one of the kids in the back of the room shouted.

"Enemies? Really, Josh? I don't believe you have any enemies." Pastor Mike laughed. "You all know what I mean. Get to know some new people—and you leaders, you know who you are. Sit with someone new."

"I wish he hadn't said that," Karrie whispered to Lo'laini. "Someone's going to come over here and act all fake sweet."

"Maybe not." Lo'laini nodded her head over Karrie's shoulder. Standing behind her were two teenage boys.

"I don't know, Tom. These girls look way too sophisticated for us," said the kid standing right behind Karrie. He was just a little taller than Lo'laini; he had coffee-brown skin and curly ebony hair. When Karrie looked up at him, his hazel-green eyes made her suddenly catch her breath.

"Well, I don't know." Lo'laini winked at Karrie. "I think we could lower our standards just for this one time."

"Here's to lowered standards," the other boy laughed. He pulled his chair around to face both of the girls. "My name is Tom, and he's Josh."

Josh had sunburnt red skin and straw like blond hair that fell over his eyes. Tom, whom Karrie had seen over Lo'laini's shoulder, had on a rust-colored T-shirt and still had his swimming trunks on from surfing with Pastor Mike that morning. Both boys pulled in seats so all four of them made a perfect circle.

"Okay." Pastor Mike picked up the wireless microphone from the platform and walked to the center of the room. "Each one of your groups should have a leader who is in possession of a shoe box. In that box are a couple things for you to work with and some Bible verses. Let me tell you what we are going to do this morning: you are going to teach Sunday school this morning, and I am going to learn from you. 'How are we going to teach Sunday school,' you may ask? You are going to use the items in your box as object lessons to teach the Bible verses. You have twenty minutes. Ready, set, go!"

The room erupted to the sound of giggles and groans as the kids tore open their boxes and examined the various items. There were scissors, colored paper, toilet paper cardboard rolls, tissue paper, cork, and foam.

"Dude, I think we're lost," said Josh, thumbing through the contents of the box.

"Let's look at the verse first," suggested Karrie as she opened her Bible.

"That looks like a well-loved Bible," said Tom.

Karrie's face warmed in a blush. "It's the Living Bible, my Sunday school teacher Miss Dawn gave it me. What verse do you want me look up?" she asked through a smile she could not hide.

"Let's just take the middle one," said Lo'laini. "Okay, Second Corinthians chapter twelve, verses seven to ten. I'll read it aloud. 'Even though I have received such wonderful revelations from God. So to keep me from becoming proud, I was given a thorn in my flesh, a messenger from Satan to torment me and keep me from becoming proud. Three different times I begged the Lord to take it away. Each time he said, "My grace is all you need. My power works best in weakness." So now I am glad to boast about my weaknesses, so that the power of Christ can work through me. That's why I take pleasure in my weaknesses, and in the insults, hardships, persecutions, and troubles that I suffer for Christ. For when I am weak, then I am strong."

While Lo'laini was reading, Tom had cut a brown piece of cardboard into a triangle. When she finished reading, he stabbed it into his chest and fell in the middle of the circle.

"Ugh." He sighed in a melodramatic moan. "Tell my Mommy that I loved her." He fell, faking death. Karrie broke out into uncontrollable laughter while Lo'laini just rolled her eyes. "Okay," said Tom, getting up from the ground, "I'll get serious. But you must say I made a good thorn."

"I think it's a great thorn," Karrie said with a smile.

"But to state the obvious," Lo'laini said coolly, "I don't think that was the kind of thorn Paul was talking about."

They all quieted down and looked at the passage again. "Like I said before, I think we're doomed," Tom whispered.

"Not that doomed," said Josh. "I think it meant something was wrong with Paul. Something physical—he was dying or something."

"You mean like we're dying here?" Tom laughed.

Lo'laini's face became serious and hard, and Karrie realized the jokes weren't funny when Tom laughed about dying. She hoped the guys would pick up on Lo'laini's mood and get a little more serious.

Then Pastor Mike stepped into the group.

"Am I right, Pastor Mike?" Josh asked, looking up at Pastor Mike. "Was Paul sick or something? Is that why he wrote that verse?"

"Maybe," said Pastor Mike.

"So that's the lesson," said Tom in a deep, serious slow voice. "We're all going to die someday."

Karrie could not help but giggle at this point. Lo'laini glared at her, and she quickly lost her smile.

"I don't think someone dying is very funny," Lo'laini said coldly. "I don't think that was the point of the verse."

"Okay, Lo'laini, what do you think the point of the verse is?" asked Pastor Mike.

"I think it was that he prayed three times," Lo'laini confidently said. "God gave him grace, but God didn't give him what he wanted. So, that's the point. Paul prayed and didn't get what he wanted."

"So the prayers didn't do anything?" Tom scratched his head looking at the Scripture.

"No," retorted Lo'laini. "The prayers did something, but not the thing he wanted them to do." Her voice was quivering, and Karrie was frightened she might lose her composure and start to cry.

Karrie knew Lo'laini was talking about her mother, but no one else did. She felt responsible for calming Lo'laini down and telling her not to take it so seriously, but she couldn't. Karrie's stomach started to hurt. She had never seen Lo'laini act this way in public, especially in front of guys. Karrie had now been at the group home for three years, and she had watched Lo'laini, and Lo'laini never got unnerved by anything. Whenever a fight erupted at the house, Lo'laini was the one who always kept her cool. Sometimes when girls came home from a court hearing or a bad visit with their parents, they would come into the house looking for a fight.

Sometimes a girl would get angry because she said someone had gotten into her stuff or stolen something, and she would come after whoever was sitting in the living room. Although all the girls' case studies were confidential, word would get around, and eventually everybody knew everyone else's business. Worst of all, they would use their abuse against each other by whispering cruel things to each other when the houseparent was out of earshot. The cruel words would never get to Lo'laini.

She would just look coldly back at the person who had said something cruel, and she would say, "You must be talking to someone else about something I don't know about, because no one talks to me that way."

The other girl would always back down. At school, no one was calmer around guys than Lo'laini. Karrie was envious of Lo'laini's façade, and she wanted to imitate it; but her emotions always showed through. Now, in this Sunday school class, Lo'laini was unraveling—over a Bible verse! She had warned Karrie not to bring the group home into church; now she was doing it!

Karrie couldn't stop Lo'laini from saying too much; she wanted to save her from embarrassment. What if Lo'laini really lost her temper and hit someone? What if she let it slip that they were living in the group home? All these kids looked so perfect, with their perfect families—what would they think? But watching Lo'laini's bottom lip tremble, Karrie realized something was happening to Lo'laini that not even she herself could stop. A painful truth was rising up inside of her that she could not stop herself from expressing, and this time the truth was more important than looking cool.

Karrie clutched her Bible and closed her eyes, not knowing what would happen next.

"Sometimes prayer acts that way," said Pastor Mike, laying his hand on Lo'laini's back. Lo'laini cracked a smile.

Suddenly Karrie calmed down. Nothing was going to happen. She looked up at Pastor Mike. A real grown-up is here. Karrie smiled to herself.

"But how do we teach that lesson with this stuff?" asked Tom.

Then Lo'laini's face brightened up. "I know!" She picked up the cardboard thorn Josh had made and taped it on Josh's chest. "This is something my friend Karrie taught me." Lo'laini picked the streams of red, yellow, green, and blue tissue paper and taped them on as though they were coming out of the thorn.

"So there is a rainbow coming out of my thorn," Josh said with a puzzled look on his face.

"A rainbow is a promise from God." Karrie smiled at Lo'laini.

"Very good," Pastor Mike patted Lo'laini on the back. "A rainbow is the covenant from God. It is the covenant of God's preservation of creation in the story of Noah."

"Yeah, but in Noah's story, creation wasn't preserved. A lot of animals drowned." Josh looked up at Pastor Mike.

"But not everything. God preserved remnants of His creation through the flood."

"So what are you trying teach us?" Pastor Mike looked a Lo'laini.

"I guess I am going to say some things do get destroyed, but not everything gets destroyed," Lo'laini whispered as she was looking at the cardboard thorn with the rainbow tissue streams clumsily taped to the edge.

"Prayer does something, but not always the things we want it to do. But it always preserves us," Pastor Mike looked proudly at the group. "I think we've got a really good lesson from this group. Someone write it down, and you can share it as we gather together as a group."

"I told you these girls were way too smart for us." Tom winked at Karrie, and she blushed again.

And God said, "This is the sign of the covenant I am making between me and you and every living creature with you, a covenant for all generations to come: I have set my rainbow in the clouds, and it will be the sign of the covenant between me and the earth. Whenever I bring clouds over the earth and the rainbow appears in the clouds, I will remember my covenant between me and you and all living creatures of every kind. Never again will the waters become a flood to destroy all life. Whenever the rainbow appears in the clouds, I will see it and remember the everlasting covenant between God and all living creatures of every kind on the earth." So God said to Noah, "This is the sign of the covenant I have established between me and all life on the earth."

—Genesis 9:11–17

Chapter 14

Karrie thought she could feel her body changing when she was eleven, but it wasn't until she was sixteen that she really felt things change. For the next two years, Karrie blossomed into young womanhood, and her body added the painful cramps of menstruation to her other worries of home and family. Her friendship with Lo'laini deepened. Lo'laini helped Karrie develop a hard exterior, while Karrie softened Lo'laini's attitude. Court dates, parental visits, and social workers' evaluations were supplemented by church youth group and church retreats. Tom found excuses to show up at school and church . . . wherever Karrie could be found. Lo'laini learned to tolerate Tom's presence on outings because Karrie adored his company. Lo'laini thought her heart would break when Karrie was placed in a foster home, but she was comforted when her social worker told her that she would be reunited with her father.

"He's really trying, Karrie," she texted Karrie after a court-appointed visit. "He's going to twelve-step groups, and he's got this new house we can live in. How's things at your new home?"

"Not bad, not good, it's just there," Karrie texted back. "Meet me after school tomorrow by the fountain. There's something I want to talk to you about."

Karrie sat by the school fountain, anxiously. She pulled the crumpled yellow paper out of her backpack her guidance counselor had given her at the beginning of the day and read it again.

"Okay, what's up?" Karrie heard Lo'laini's voice boom over. Lo'laini flung down her backpack on the bench next to the water fountain and lay down on the grass. "Hey, where's our third wheel? What's that boy's name? Tomb? Todd? Ted? Taint?"

"Tom." Karrie rolled her eyes and sat down on edge of the fountain. "He's at track practice."

"Oh, what a shame." Lo'laini smiled "It's not that I don't like being around him—it's just really that I don't."

"Thanks for sharing." Karrie poked Lo'laini in the ribs with her toe which made Lo'laini sit up. "What is up, Lo'laini, is that we won!"

"We won?" asked Lo'laini. "What did we win?"

"The contest!" Karrie laughed. "You remember? Your mom's apple cheese-cake recipe? The one I entered with Career Center so we could get a paid internship this summer?" Karrie showed Lo'laini the crumbled yellow paper, and Lo'laini snatched it out of her hand.

"This is so cool!" Lo'laini held it up overhead and yelled. "We won! Yeah, losers! We—Karrie and me—won, which means you all lost. Money, money, money, we're going to have money this summer!" Both girls leaned back and laughed. "So when do we start?" asked Lo'laini.

"Next Saturday," said Karrie. "Let me read the letter."

Lo'laini handed the letter back to Karrie and lay down on the bench next to her with her hand cupped beneath her head. "It says here we'll pick up our uniforms from the career center and show up at eight in the morning for brief training next Saturday. Then they will introduce us to the staff at their ten o'clock meeting, and we'll serve the dessert at a noon luncheon."

"What kind of luncheon?" asked Lo'laini.

"It's a funeral repast." Karrie paused for a moment and then looked at Lo'laini. "Okay, that's a little morbid, serving your mom's recipe at a funeral repast. You're okay with it, aren't you?"

"Not too morbid, if I get paid." Lo'laini laughed. "I mean, if it's a large fam-ily funeral, people are going to want to sit around talk, and while they talk, they are going to want to eat. So I think that'll be good exposure." Lo'laini sat up again and looked at Karrie. "Anyway, I am glad it is next Saturday and not this Saturday, because this Saturday"—Lo'laini paused—"I'm moving back with my dad!"

"Oh, Lo'laini," Karrie squealed. "Congrats. I'm so happy for you." Both girls hugged, and then Karrie sat down again to look at the piece of paper while Lo'laini lay back down on the bench. "It feels so good—to be going home, I mean."

"Yeah, I can't even imagine that in my life right now."

"How are things going between you and your mom, Kar?"

"They're okay, I guess. I'm trying not to let her manipulate me anymore. We're still meeting and talking. That can't be bad." Karrie held the paperback up to the sunlight. "You know, Lo'laini, this is the first time I've ever won anything in my life."

"So maybe this will be new trend, girl." Lo'laini picked up her backpack. "I'm going to be late. I got soccer practice today."

"A new trend," Karrie whispered to herself. "I'd like that. I hope so."

Two weeks later, Karrie and Lo'laini found themselves in the midst of adult servers and cooks at a La Jolla restaurant that neither of the girls would ever have even dreamed of entering as a customer. The manager was giving a lecture before the repast started. The eyes of the servers at the upscale beachfront restaurant followed their well-dressed boss, Alejandro Rodriguez, as he walked back and forth between the servers in the back kitchen. He was dressed in a dark suit with a light-blue shirt and a black silk tie. He had a small pearl pin that held his tie carefully in place. His dark hair was neatly combed to one side. His posture and tone of voice carried the authority that made his employees take notice.

The servers wore simple white button-down shirts and black tuxedo slacks, with a simple white apron that was neatly draped across their waist. "Today we have a funeral repast in the back room at the restaurant, as well as a full house in the front. Now there's a reason why twenty percent of our profits come from funeral repasts—families trust us with their privacy and that we will treat their meal with dignity. So, servers," Alejandro went on to say, "you are going to be so slick, so professional that no one in that party will know you are there. No one will know their glasses are being filled—they will be filled before they notice they are empty. The water pitchers on tables, as well as the fresh bread baskets, will never be allowed to become empty. There are four courses, but no conversations between family members will be interrupted between courses. This family and their guests will be able to cry, laugh, and comfort each other while being served without interruption. We've set up an entrance in the back, with decorative lighting, and Anthony is going to be the doorman tonight.

"Our repast guests will be entering from the back door, nearest to the parking lot to protect their mood and to give them a quiet evening amid the celebratory mood in the front. So I want everyone to be on their toes tonight and to keep the kitchen humming all night long. This is a four hour shift, so no breaks . . . "

Karrie whispered to Lo'laini, "The button on top of my slacks just popped off. Do you have a safety pin?"

"No!" gasped Lo'laini. "What are you going to do? Wait a minute; I have a bobby pin. Let's see if I can make that work." Lo'laini pulled a bobby pin out of her hair and bent one-half of it downward to make a hook. She stuck one side of the pin through the buttonhole in the back of Karrie's cummerbund at the top of her slacks and hooked the half of the pin into a loose thread loop on the inside of the cummerbund. "I don't think it'll hold, but it's the best I think we can do for right now," Lo'laini whispered.

Then they were both startled by the booming voice of Alejandro. "I want to introduce two of our guest cooks tonight from the advanced culinary class in their high school. This is Lo'laini and Karrie."

Both girls looked up and forced a casual smile.

"They will be preparing apple cheesecake bars as dessert. Because both of them would like the privilege of working with us this summer, unlike our other guest from the high school, they will be staying behind after they finish preparing dessert to work in the kitchen. They will be helping the dishwashers and making sure the waitress stations are well supplied with fresh napkins, salt, pepper, other condiments."

"Miguel,"—Alejandro nodded his head toward a man leaning against the back wall of kitchen with an unlit cigarette hanging from his mouth—"did you walk them through the steps of server's station and dishwashing protocol?"

Miguel nodded back at Alejandro. "Sure did."

"Yeah, I'd like to walk him through a few steps, that jerk," whispered Lo'laini.

Karrie elbowed her. "Shhh, don't mess this up."

"So, there is something I like to say to my bus boys that I wish to tell you, too," Alejandro said, smiling at the two girls. "As owner, I am depending on the chefs to make the meal appetizing enough to create a successful evening. The chefs are dependent on servers to make the dining experience pleasurable. The servers are dependent on the kitchen staff to make sure they are supplied with the instruments they need to make a dining experience pleasurable. So you might say this evening's success is dependent upon you two."

The rest of the servers laughed politely. Lo'laini and Karrie stood as still as statues with polite smiles still plastered across their faces.

"You two girls need some help?" whispered a short, motherly-looking server standing behind them.

"Yes," said Karrie. "My button popped."

"Come into the back room with me. I'll fix it," said the server.

"But Mr. Rodriguez hasn't finished his speech yet, and I don't want to get into trouble."

"Don't worry about Mr. Rodriguez. My name is Isabella Rodriguez, and you won't get into any trouble." Isabella walked them into the back room behind the kitchen, where she opened a locker and pulled out a small plastic bag with pins, needle and thread, and small scissors. Karrie started to take her pants off when Isabella stopped her. "No need for that. I can do this on with your pants still on you. I've done it before, and I'll do again. You're not the only server whose pants haven't held up." Isabella gently yanked on the back of Karrie's pants and began to stitch the button back on again. "So, I noticed you two girls really seem to take care of each other. Have you known each other for a long time?"

"We've been friends for two years." Lo'laini smiled at Isabella. "We met at a very exclusive camp one summer."

"Well," Isabella cut the thread and buttoned up Karrie's pants again, "we are honored to be in your presence." She made a slight bow. Karrie cracked a smile at Lo'laini, who shrugged her shoulders.

"So is Mr. Rodriguez your brother? And does your family really own the restaurant?" asked Karrie.

"Mr. Rodriguez is my husband. Sorry about the joke out there about everything being dependent on you two—of course, it is not. He just wants you to take the job seriously. So if you keep yourselves busy, make sure your stations are clean, he'll likely hire you. He just wants everyone to keep in mind we are all here to work, not to socialize." Isabella turned Karrie around to take a look at her handiwork. She smiled and nodded her head in approval as she looked up and down at the slacks. As she was leaving the room, she looked over her shoulder at Lo'laini and said, "If Miguel gives you any trouble, you talk to me. He's on probation for other rude remarks he has made to women servers here. You're right, he is a jerk, but he's a good head chef and manages the kitchen even better, so after the guests arrive, listen to him. He'll direct you appropriately. I'll make sure of that."

"Exclusive camp! Really, Lo'laini?"

"I was trying to impress her!"

"You noticed that didn't work, right?" Karrie laughed.

"Okay, everyone on the repast team, stations, please, the evening has begun." Alejandro looked over his shoulder while peering out a window as a couple of sleek black sedan cars pulled up into the parking lot. "We cleared off a sideboard for both you girls." Miguel nodded his head toward the side counter while carefully watching over three different skillets simmering over the open flames on the corner stove. "You got everything you need—ingredients, cutting board, sink, and, of course, knives. Be careful with those knives, okay? They're on lend, and they're not cheap. Even though I already know you are going to chop like a bunch of wannabe housewives."

Miguel's last remark rang like a challenge in Lo'laini's ears. "So, he doesn't think I can handle a kitchen knife?" she whispered to Karrie.

She walked briskly to the back cutting table and placed all the apples in the strainer and ran them under cold running water. Then she began to swiftly peel and core the apples with a paring knife. Not once did her paring knife blade leave the skin of the apple as the peels gently spiraled off each of the round fruits. Then she grabbed a chopping knife in one hand and held a small slice of the apple in the other. Her knife fell in quick small chopping succession on the cutting board, leaving perfectly shaped apple slices while she pushed the apples gently under the blade of the knife.

"Dude," said one of the chef assistants, looking intently at Miguel, "did you see that kid cut?"

Miguel shrugged his shoulders.

"Very impressive," said Alejandro, who had just entered the kitchen from the main floor. "Karrie, let the food processer do the work. Don't bother mixing ingredients before they hit the food processor."

Karrie blushed but tried to conceal her embarrassment by quickly following orders. She stopped mixing the cream cheese, eggs, butter, and sugar and poured the contents of her bowl into a nearby food processor.

"I know that's the way they taught you at school," said Alejandro, "but we just do things differently here."

"If you want to mix ingredients by hand, wait for the crust and crumb topping. Those ingredients will work best if you use a fork to blend them together," said Isabella from over the counter as she picked up a couple of plates of crab-stuffed jalapeno pepper appetizers.

"Hey!" shouted Miguel, "whose kitchen is this anyway? Both of you, out front! You do your job and I'll do mine!"

Alejandro shrugged, putting both hands up. "Okay, Miguel, just keep an eye on everything." And he walked out of the kitchen to greet the customers.

The kitchen was buzzing with activity. The window nearest to Lo'laini and Karrie was serving the dining room out front. The counter quickly filled with gracefully plated food of shellfish, empanadas, tender beef wrapped in crisp flour tortillas, and salsa and sour cream–drenched nachos. As soon as the servers grabbed the plates, new plates appeared in a constant flow. A light level of conversation and laughter could be faintly heard from the front of the restaurant. The other counter was for the repast in the back dining room. The food was quietly taken out on carts with each course following the others. Gracefully plated chicken dinners, crab and shrimp tacos, and steaming plates of picadillo-ground beef dish with tomatoes, olives, and raisins filled those carts. Soft music, and even quieter conversation, could be heard from the other room. The chefs' eyes didn't leave their pots and skillets—unless only occasionally to look up to shout to the servers which order was up.

The clang of the dishwasher could be heard over all the activity, and it rattled like a drum keeping the beat for the entire kitchen crew as they worked together like a well-rehearsed dance routine. Karrie smiled as she finished rolling out the crust, right on time. She laid it out on a large lightly greased cookie sheet and then lightly sprayed the pastry with a thin layer of butter. Then she sprinkled it with sugar, cinnamon, nutmeg, and cornstarch. Then she spread a layer of the cream cheese mixture on the pastry.

Next, Lo'laini gently laid thin apple slices over the cream cheese mixture. On top of the apples, she sprinkled cinnamon, sugar, and cornstarch. For the final touch, they both spooned on the crumb topping, which was made up of butter, brown sugar, and flour.

"Okay, it looks like you two are done with the dessert," Miguel said to the pair as they finished sprinkling on the crumb topping. "Your next job is the server stations." He pointed to two stations on the outside of each of the counters. "Don't worry too much about the condiments. They're well stocked. Your big job for the night is to make sure there are clean glasses and utensils the bus boys and servers can grab quickly and that there are pitchers of ice water where the servers and bus boys can get when needed. When you're not stocking the server stations, you need to keep an eye on the dirty dishes on the carts from the repast. They'll start to stack up pretty quickly later in evening. Just make sure the dishes get to the dishwashing counters, so the guys in the back can grab them quickly. Then wipe off the cart and place it by the chef's counter so they can plate the next courses."

"Hey, wait a minute!" said Lo'laini. "Don't we get to plate the dessert?"

"Sorry, babe." Miguel winked at Lo'laini. "Only the chef plates dishes in the professional restaurants. I guess you'll have to wait to practice that activity in one of your classes *at school*. Meanwhile, most of your evening here will be spent running back and forth from the kitchen to the server stations making sure everything is in stock and clearing away dirty dishes from the counters."

Lo'laini started to grit her teeth when Miguel winked at them. Karrie elbowed her to let her know Alejandro was watching them.

"Look, why don't you girls take five minutes," said Alejandro. "Take a bathroom break. Things won't be picking up for about ten minutes, so now's a good time to take a break. Miguel, I need to talk to you."

Karrie and Lo'laini walked out the side door. When they opened the door, a burst of ocean wind bathed their faces, blowing back their hair and cooling the nervous sweat from the night's work.

"Boy," said Karrie wiping off her face with a cool towel, "I didn't realize how hot that kitchen was until we came out here."

"No," Lo'laini said, "I knew that kitchen was pretty hot. Near the end, it was getting so hot I could barely stand it. So now I finally understand the statement, 'If you can't stand the heat, get out of the kitchen.'"

"Thanks for not losing it." Karrie looked up at Lo'laini.

"I guess there are people like that all over the crummy world." Lo'laini sighed as she leaned up against the back wall. From where they were standing, they could see the repast party through the back room's glass-plated wall. The room was filled with people—some sitting around the table and others standing in clusters, lightly laughing while others held on to each other talking in quiet confidence.

At the front of the room was a picture of a young black sailor in a formal uniform with an American flag draped in the background. Seated at the front table were two older couples, holding each other's hands tightly as if they feared if they let go, they would lose their partner. A younger woman sat at the end of the table, apart from the two couples, gracefully greeting people as they came up to the table to pay their respects.

People were taking turns coming up to the head table to hug and whisper kind greetings to the two couples; but most people seemed to spend more time with the young woman.

"You can always tell when it's a family." Lo'laini wistfully watched the people inside the room interact with one another. "Because the babies are always the stars of the show."

She was right. Four infant car seats were being passed around the room among the crowd. The car seats each held a cooing baby, who was being greeted with "oohs" and "ahhs" by family members. Three toddlers wobbling around the room were being worshiped by the elderly ladies wearing large-brimmed hats. The women gloated with pride as they recognized the child's parent in the toddler's smile, unsteady walk, or voice.

Unbeknownst to the toddler, their mere existence brought immeasurable joy to the women. Each child's resemblance inspired a familiar memory of a previous child from another time. In every conversation and interaction, something was being embraced, and something was being passed down to the next generation. The family scene made Karrie sick with yearning. Then something startled her.

"Hey . . . " She nudged Lo'laini. "Did you recognize the lady at the end of the table?"

"No way," said Lo'laini. "I can't believe that's . . . "

"Miss Sophia!" they said in unison. They both squinted to make sure. It was the same Miss Sophia from the group home, although she looked and acted different than she used to. She wasn't wearing her familiar jeans and T-shirt, and she did not have a book in her hand, nor was her hair in dreadlocks. She had on a fitted dark blue suit with silver buttons that shone from across the room. A string of pearls graced her long neck, and her hair was made up in tiny braids that hung eloquently over her shoulders like a regal Egyptian wig from the age of the pharaohs.

"Wow, she sure looks different," said Karrie.

"Yeah," said Lo'laini. "The difference between work clothes and church clothes, I guess."

"Or the difference being with family or being at work." Karrie moved closer to look at Miss Sophia. "Do you think she still remembers us?"

"I don't think so. There were a lot of girls in that house, so she couldn't have remembered us all. She took care of a lot of girls." Lo'laini's voice tapered off as they both continued to stare at Miss Sophia. They were both mesmerized by her elegant presence while she was greeting the guests who were coming up to her.

"Hey, do you think the sailor was her fiancé?" Lo'laini pointed to the picture at the front of the room.

"I don't know," said Karrie. "I think that is the guy I saw on her laptop one time I was at that house. When I asked her who it was, she told me it was none of my business."

"Yeah." Lo'laini turned her face away from the restaurant to catch the ocean breeze. The stress from preparing the dessert was beginning to fade. She smiled at Karrie. "You know she wasn't being snotty by saying that. There was a rule that we weren't supposed to know anything about the houseparent's personal lives."

"I know," replied Karrie. "But she did share some stuff with me that first night that made me wish I could know her family."

"There was another reason she might have told you it was none of your business. It was because it wasn't any of your business." Miguel smiled at the girls as they startled at the sound of his voice and turned around to see his intruding face. "You guys are back on the clock. No stalking guests, huh?"

Both girls glanced at each other, wondering how much Miguel heard or how he might use it against them. However, once back in the kitchen, both flew into action. They moved quickly from the dishwashing counter to push back the freshly wiped carts to the chef's counter to check back to the server's stations. Everything that could be wiped clean was wiped clean, and everything that should be stocked was stocked. They only occasionally paused to make pleasant conversation with the servers or dishwashers.

Alejandro and Isabella occasionally glanced approvingly in their direction. Then suddenly, the evening was over. Busboys were pulling tablecloths and napkins off the tables and throwing them into large laundry carts. Weary servers were seated at tables counting their tips. Alejandro and Isabella were counting the day's profits in the back room. The dishwashers started rapping a Caribbean song using wooden spoons to beat on the counters while they put away the last of the silverware.

Karrie and Lo'laini sat down near the server station after they finished stocking for the next morning. The servers gathered around the station to talk about restaurant gossip; one of the servers had just gotten engaged. The girls chattered about dresses, flowers, and reception venues. Lo'laini and Karrie felt as if they had been briefly invited into the adult world, and it felt wonderful.

"Do you girls have someone to pick you up?" asked Isabella as she put away a large ledger in the back locker.

"Yes," said Karrie. "I texted my foster mom to pick me up, and Lo'laini's dad is coming down after his meeting."

"Yeah." Lo'laini looked coldly at Karrie. "We're meeting them outside."

As they walked outside, Lo'laini sighed exasperatedly at Karrie. "Don't tell everyone everything!"

"What do you mean?"

"'My foster parent'? Just say my aunt or my mom or something!" Lo'laini sighed, looking back Karrie. "And my dad's meeting? It won't take much for Isabella to ask what kind of meeting it was, and what do you think she'll think of me if she finds out it is AA?"

"Isabella seems really nice. I don't think she'd hold it against you. I know I could never call my foster mother my mom or aunt." She was going to say more, but then Lo'laini nudged her and tilted her head to the side so Karrie could see Miguel. He was standing in the corner behind the kitchen door. The glow of his cigarette had suddenly made him visible to the two girls.

"Let's wait 'til we get closer to the parking lot," said Lo'laini as she pulled Karrie away. As they walked into the parking lot, they could see Miss Sophia standing by two older women who were talking to her. Her car door was open as if she was about to get in her car when one of the women had stopped her to talk to her.

"Do you think we should go up and talk to her?" asked Karrie.

"Let's walk by her slowly. If she recognizes us, then we'll talk to her. If not, we'll just walk on to stand by the sidewalk while we wait for our rides." Lo'laini took Karrie's arm and they started to walk toward Miss Sophia, but as they approached the black sedan, one of the women hugged Miss Sophia and walked away. Miss Sophia leaned against the other woman, her forehead wrinkled up, and she began to cry.

"He's gone, Mama. He's gone." Miss Sophia sobbed.

"Not all gone, child. He's just got a different address," consoled the older woman.

"But he's been in a different place for so long . . . so much so that I was beginning to think he wasn't really real. But I always thought it was okay because I would see him again and then I would know he was real, that we were real, and we'd have a home together! There was so much I wanted to tell him when he came home. Now I know he'll never come home. Now he's where I can never see him again. I cannot touch him, I can't hear his voice, and I can't tell him I'm sorry—so sorry about all the stupid things that kept us apart." Miss Sophia's tears turned to sobs.

"But now he's in a place where he is comforted. He's not at war anymore," said the older woman as she wrapped her arms around Miss Sophia and gently rocked her. "As a Christian woman, I know right now I should be telling you one day you'll see him again and we'll all be at home together, but right now, all I can say is that I think there are too many tears here on this earth."

"It hurts, Mama," Miss Sophia wept. "It hurts so badly that sometimes I can't breathe."

"So maybe you need a place where you can breathe for a while. Come back home. I'm not saying forever, but for a couple of months until some of the pain is not so strong." The older women held Miss Sophia's face and looked directly into her eyes.

Miss Sophia nodded her head, and they embraced again. "This world is just too full of tears, sweetheart. Just too many tears," said Miss Sophia's mother.

Karrie and Lo'laini stood about five feet from them. They were far enough away from the restaurant lights that they were still cloaked in darkness, so Miss Sophia could not see them, but they were close enough that they heard the intimate conversation between a mother and child. Karrie and Lo'laini could neither move nor speak as they reverently watched this bittersweet moment of a mother's love for her child.

Chapter 15

"Hey, Miguel!" Alejandro's voice from behind them startled them, so they turned around to face the restaurant. "You're off the clock, why don't you just go home?"

"I'm just watching the kiddies while they wait for their folks." Miguel's face suddenly appeared from behind the restaurant. His gaze startled Karrie and Lo'laini.

"Go home, Miguel, I'm going to take a break with my lady. We'll watch the girls."

Isabella walked out of the restaurant and joined her husband on the side porch. Alejandro draped his arm around her and handed her a glass of wine, and the couple sat together on an iron bench that leaned against the restaurant wall. Miguel slowly walked away toward the parking lot as a spiral of white cigarette smoke rose above his head.

Lo'laini pulled Karrie back away from the parking lot.

"We're going to wait by the ocean," she said over her shoulder as they walked by Alejandro and Isabella. They both took off their shoes. The sand was wet and cold from the night air. They walked toward the edge of the ocean and sat down on the wet sand. The ocean's white-topped waves glowed in night sky, and soon they could feel small waves ebb against their feet.

"Both of those girls' pants are going to be soaking wet before their parents arrive," they heard Isabella laugh from behind them.

"So, someone will do the laundry," Alejandro replied.

"She's right, you know," said Lo'laini. "Why don't you text your foster mom and say you're spending the night. Then you don't have worry about her having one of her hissy fits over her car."

Karrie laughed and pulled out her phone. Within minutes, her foster mom replied with a brief text: "Okay. Make sure you're home by noon on Saturday." She showed Lo'laini her phone.

"That is the coldest woman I've ever met," said Lo'laini while scooting her body deeper in the sand.

"What do you mean?" asked Karrie.

"She knew the school set up this opportunity for you to try out our recipe at a real restaurant tonight and how excited you were," Lo'laini said, "but she doesn't ask anything about it."

"What questions should she have asked?"

"Real parents ask questions like, 'How'd it go? Did your boss like you?'" Lo'laini sat up to look Karrie in the eye. "A real parent would have showed up tonight, just to see you work, even if it was just out of the corner of their eye while they sat eating in front."

"When your dad came earlier to get a cup coffee and watched you, you said he embarrassed you."

"Yeah, he embarrasses me all the time," said Lo'laini, "but it's better being embarrassed than being left alone."

"Well, if my foster mom did ask about work tonight," Karrie nestled down in the sand, "I would say we were hot and slick and that they'd be a fool not to hire us."

They gave each other a high five, and then they both lay down in the sand to stare at the stars. "So I guess you can see why I can't call Mrs. Wilson my mom? Not even if I am just pretending for someone."

"Yeah, I do. But you've gotta figure out a way to disguise who she is so people don't know."

"I guess it doesn't bother me if people know."

"Well, it bothers me! Karrie, when people know this kind of stuff, they will use it against you. They treat you different after they know. They take advantage of you! They try to make you look bad so that they look good. You know they do, Karrie, and it's not good. Even at church, they do it."

Karrie looked back at the ocean, and they were quiet for a while as they listened to the soft roar of the waves.

"I'm telling you this, Karrie, because I know Pastor Mike asked you to share your testimony in church," said Lo'laini. "Be careful girl, that's all I'm saying."

"But lots of people share hard stuff in their testimony. I thought that was the point? I mean, aren't we supposed to talk about how Jesus saved us from the rough stuff?"

"Yeah, but those people always end up saying that they accepted Jesus and things changed in a moment. Both you and I had the bad stuff happen to us after we accepted Christ. People can get real mean about those things when stuff happens that way. Besides, you're a girl, and people treat girls different than guys when they talk about this stuff. Remember when that lady started to whack you around when you came forward to have someone pray with you at camp?"

"She wasn't whacking me," laughed Karrie. "She was laying hands on me. She said she was casting out the spirit of abuse from me." Karrie rolled her eyes.

"Karrie, she was knocking the stuff out of you! I remember it. I remember when she called it the spirit of Jezebel ruling over you! Man, did that creep me out! I don't know what she was really casting out of you. Your pain? Or was she trying to get *you* out of you? It didn't make sense to me then, and it doesn't make sense to me now. I swore if she hit you one more time and said. 'In the name of Jesus,' I was going get up and slap her back. If Pastor Mike didn't step in, I would have! Who was Jezebel anyway?"

"Pastor Mike said she was an Old Testament queen who tried to steal some land to please her husband," said Karrie. "I still can't figure out what that has to do with abuse. But I thought it was pretty cool how Pastor Mike got up and stood between us and started to pray. No one has ever protected me that way!"

"I remember . . ." Lo'laini laughed. " . . . how she turned red and stormed out. Everyone was so quiet after that. No one knew what to do, and I've never seen Christian grown-ups fight with each other at a church meeting."

"Well, they didn't fight," said Karrie. "Pastor Mike just stood in front of her, and she turned around and walked out."

"Oh girl, you know there was a fight simmering under each of them. But they just didn't show it."

Lo'laini and Karrie started to laugh, and then Karrie said, "Later, Pastor Mike told me that Jezebel had nothing to do with my nightmares. He said that lady probably couldn't handle the fact that sometimes bad things happen to Christians—that's why she put on that show. He said he thought she was trying to beat back her own memories in that prayer over me." Karrie sat up and pushed her toes into the wet sand.

"That's what I'm saying, Karrie. Some people can't handle that bad things happen to Christians, so they try to make you look bad, like you're not a Christian, or you're just a bad one."

"I guess," said Karrie, lying back in the sand.

"So why do you want to talk about it, Karrie?" asked Lo'laini.

"I don't want to talk about it. It's just what happened to me. I mean, that's what we're supposed to share, isn't it? We're supposed to share what Jesus saved us from . . ."

"Except, Jesus didn't really save you from it, did He? I mean, you were already a Christian when it happened." Lo'laini lay down to look up at the sky.

"Yeah, but He helps me through it. I guess I want to share about it, because I think it helps," said Karrie. "It's like what Miss Dawn, my Sunday school teacher said—you either get better, or bitter."

"So we just got two choices?" said Lo'laini. "I hate it when people say things like that. They take something that is complicated and try to make it easy when it's not. 'You can be bitter or better'—that's like saying you have two holidays, Christmas or Easter, when there's a whole lot of holidays in between those two."

"What are you talking about?" Karrie laughed. "Girl, now you're the one talking crazy."

"I'm just saying," Lo'laini said throwing her hands up in the air, " Maybe you can be better and a little angry too or be at your worst while you're getting better and feel a whole lot ways in-betweens."

Lo'laini's voice softened. "Karrie, you just can't trust everyone. I guess that's what I'm saying. I know there are nice people like Miss Dawn and Pastor Will who want to help, but there are some real mean people, like that woman at camp. And the scary thing is they don't know they are mean. They'll use it against you, Karrie, you know they will, so you got to watch out."

The ocean tide was creeping up to their knees now, so Lo'laini and Karrie scooted backward a couple of feet. Karrie realized she had touched a nerve with Lo'laini, so she was quiet for a while before she spoke. "So how are things with your dad?"

"Pretty good, I guess, since he's been going to his AA meetings," Lo'laini said as she lay back into the sand again. "I like the new condo we got after he got his old job back. I know I got angry when my case manager first said I should consider moving back in with him, but I was glad in the end because he still wanted me to live with him. I really do like living with my dad. It is so much better than foster care. Although, he seems a lot sadder now that he's sober." Lo'laini was quiet for a moment, and then she sat half up, leaning on her elbows, and looked at Karrie. "Karrie, don't ever tell anyone I said this, but sometimes there is a piece of me that misses my drunk dad.

"When he was drunk, he was really funny, and he didn't mope around as much. Now, he cries sometimes, late at night, when he thinks I'm asleep, and I can hear him say my mom's name. His nightmares about the war have come back, and he walks around the house late at night. He never did that when he was drinking."

Lo'laini lay back down in the sand and sighed. "But I love my sober dad because he's safer. I don't have to worry about his stoned friends showing up at the house or the police knocking down the doors. I recently met my aunts from England, and I found that we didn't meet them before this because they didn't want anything to do with my dad, even before Mom died. Yup, that's something else I found out about. When Dad decided to move in with me, the social worker made him write me a bunch of letters called 'truth telling.' Dad had been using and getting stoned for a long time, even before he met my mom. He started while he was in Afghanistan. It was kind of a relief to know my mom's death didn't cause my dad's using, but it also kind of ticked me off that he made it look that way."

"Are you ever sorry you moved back with him?" asked Karrie.

"No," said Lo'laini, "because being with my dad is being home. He always was home to me, drunk or sober. When my aunts get together with us for the holidays, it is a little bit like those people at the repast this evening. I can't believe it's been five years since I've been visiting with him and talking about this stuff, but we're okay!"

Both girls lay quiet as the cool ocean wind bathed their aching bodies from the night's work. "Hey, Kar, remember how mean I was to you when I came back from juvenile court?"

Karrie joined her friend, scooting her body so it would sink into the sand. "Yeah, I remember. I thought you were going to kick my butt. You busting into our room, screaming at me because I hadn't taken out my laundry yet."

"I thought I said you stole something," Lo'laini said with a smile. "Anyway, good thing Miss Sophia came in when she did."

"Yeah, she always seemed to make everything better—her and Miss Ellen. They made things better just by being in the room." Karrie picked up some sand and let it slip through her fingers. "It really hurt me tonight to see Miss Sophia and her mom like that this evening."

"Yeah, she really looked like she was hurting. I've never seen her like that," Lo'laini said.

"No, that's not what hurt me. It hurt because I saw she had a mom that would act that way when she was hurting."

"You don't think your mom would comfort you like that if you lost someone you loved?"

"Yeah, she'd comfort me, maybe, for that moment." Karrie wiped her face, which was now was smeared with tears and sand. "But later, she'd use it against me. That was just something that she'd do. She would be nice until my dad or Pete came home, and when they'd get angry at me, she'd join in."

"Angry for what?" asked Lo'laini.

"They'd get mad at me for anything and everything. They'd get mad when I did something good because they said I was too proud and that I was throwing it in their face. They'd get mad at me because I didn't do something the way they thought I should. My family's got this thing. They don't want to sound corny by showing affection, so they make stupid jokes about things that aren't funny. It starts out like we're on some sitcom making sarcastic putdowns on each other. Then it turns this ugly corner, and they would all start screaming like some soap opera! They would act like they were doing me a favor by setting me straight. It hurts, especially when they bring up what my dad did to me."

"And your mom didn't defend you?" asked Lo'laini.

"No, not when they are in the room. I mean, she can be nice to me when they're gone, but the moment Dad or Pete came into the room, she would join them in yelling cruel things at me and calling me ugly names. I think she's terrified she might be left out and the ugly words would turn on her if she doesn't join in, so she'd yell those things at me. I'm the one she throws under the bus to keep all the rest of them happy. They all start yelling and swearing.

First, they yell. Then someone would knock something down, and something gets broken, and then the hitting begins."

Karrie's voice tapered off as she looked out into the ocean. "I hate being hit," she whispered.

Lo'laini stood up to brush off the sand from her uniform. "Gracious, Karrie, you always let me do all the talking and complaining. I knew what your dad did, but I didn't think your mom was that cruel or that you felt so alone there. You must hate her when she does those things."

"That's the problem," said Karrie. "I don't hate her. I love her. Sometimes she can be nice and kind. She's my favorite person when she's that way. But she doesn't stay that way for long. The only reason I am talking about it now is that I have to go to court Monday. My mom appealed to the court so I could move back into her house. We're going to counseling now, Mom and me. Funny, my brothers were so mad at me because they said I was the one who told the police and my mom didn't deserve to be punished. Now they don't want anything to do with Mom or me anymore. So it's just her and me that are going to counseling." Karrie got up and bushed herself off. "You know, Lo'laini, I keep thinking it doesn't matter that I don't have a real family, because I'm okay by myself. But then I see something like we saw tonight. All those people in that room hugging each other, and the way Miss Sophia's mom hugged her, and I realize I need some kind of family."

"So what are you going to do?" asked Lo'laini.

"I don't know. I love my home, and I'm homesick, but I don't want to go back to that. I guess that I'm just going to go to court Monday and try not to cry so they don't treat me like a big baby."

Lo'laini's phone beeped, and she looked at the screen and shook out her shoes and put them back on her feet. "Dad's in the parking lot, let's go."

Both girls walked over the lumpy sand toward the parking lot. Lo'laini's father stood by his car with two ice cream cones in one hand, and he held a sign in the other hand in big black letters that read, "For the Working Women."

Lo'laini blushed and smiled. "Now, that's an embarrassing spectacle." Then she stopped and turned to Karrie. "It's not perfect, but it's home. I don't know what you should do, but there's something about being at home that I could never find in foster care."

"I get what you're saying," said Karrie.

"Hey, these cones are melting all over my arm. I know you guys can walk faster than that!" said Lo'laini's dad.

Lo'laini and Karrie kicked off their shoes and ran toward Lo'laini's dad. As they did, Lo'laini's dad started to talk like a sports announcer. "And they're rounding around first base, second base . . . third base, and the crowd goes wild as they are heading into home. And now they're safe!" Lo'laini's dad was waving his arms and laughing.

Chapter 16

In La Jolla, California, the month of February often conjures up a wet fog from the ocean, which creeps inland while bringing with it a cold mist that blankets the peninsula. Such a fog engulfed the bus stop on the dark street where Karrie anxiously waited the twenty minutes until the next bus came that would take her home from work. The grey white fog teased her fears, hiding every face that passed her on the dark street outside the restaurant. It dampened her sweater and chilled her to the bone. She softly sung a praise song under her breath as each pair of white head lights pierced through the fog whizzing by her, while she remembered every horror news story about what can happen to teenage girls when they were in the wrong place at the wrong time and were found by the wrong person.

Karrie opened her school folder and pretended to be reading, even though it was too dark to read anything. She thought if she looked like she was busy, people were more likely to leave her alone.

Finally, two large white lights flooded darkness and Karrie could hear the high-pitched brakes of a bus as it slowed to a stop. It heaved out a moan as the doors swung open before her, and she climb aboard and sat directly behind the bus driver. Last night an older homeless man had sat directly across from her. He was wearing torn faded jeans that opened under his legs to reveal he had no underwear on. He sprawled out his legs and leeringly smiled at her. His smile had frozen her in her seat and it took her a while to speak up. When she had, the bus driver threw him off the bus. She had trembled all the way home and wondered why it had taken her so long to speak up.

Karrie bit the side of her check and showed the hardest face she could muster so no one would see any fear in her. But she was afraid, and she felt alone.

It's worth it. This job gives me my own money and maybe a future. Anyway, it's better than sitting in that plastic house.

That was the name Karrie had given to her foster home, the *plastic house*. As a little girl Karrie had seen a toy plastic house on a high shelf at Walmart. She could see through the clear plastic wrap and spied a rug on the floor of the house that looked like pink cotton, and there was a vine in a small vase t covered with pink little blossoms by an overstuffed couch. It was so pretty, she had wanted to touch everything in the house. She wanted to smell everything, which she was sure smelt like fresh roses. Even though she wouldn't admit it to anyone, she even wanted to taste everything because the furniture sparkled as if it were sugar coated. She had asked her mother if she could have the house for Christmas. For days, Karrie daydreamed about how she would play with the house when it was her own. Whenever she and her mother visited Walmart, Karrie would run to the toy aisle and find the plastic house.

When she'd received the house on Christmas morning, she tore off the plastic cover and thrust her fingers inside the house and tapped them on the wooden floor. A weight of disappointment overshadowed her when she discovered the wooden floors were nothing more than painted plastic lined by a black marker. Her heart sank when she discovered the soft carpet pricked her fingers with a jagged plastic edge and her fingers crushed the overstuffed couch that was nothing more than a cardboard cutout.

"What's wrong honey? It's what you wanted, wasn't it?" Karrie's mother asked as she squatted beside her.

"Yeah," said Karrie, "it's just not what I thought it was."

"What did you think that it was?" asked her mother.

"I thought it was real," Karrie mumbled under her breath.

"It is real!" said Karrie's mother, "I mean, I paid real money for it!"

"I mean . . . more real," Karrie commented trying to soothe her mother's anger.

"Just no pleasing you girl!" Karrie's mother stood, walked out of room, and slammed her bedroom door behind her.

A lot of things seemed to turn out that way for Karrie in life. Something would seem real until she touched it, then it would turn into cruel plastic. So, Karrie had started to label things that faded before her eyes and stole her dreams and affections as *plastic*.

The Wilsons' home was the most plastic thing she had ever touched.

When Miss Ellen had first introduced Karrie to Dianne Wilson, Mrs. Wilson looked perfect. Not a hair on her head was out of place. She had a modest turned up smile that was not too broad but not too faint, her lips were perfectly lined with pink lipstick. Her brown curly hair framed her peach-hued face like a spring bonnet. Her round blue eyes smiled with approval when she first saw Karrie.

"What a pretty little girl," Miss Wilson said as Karrie entered the room.

When Karrie saw the Wilsons' house, she thought she had finally found her happy ending. The white stucco house was accented with a green tiled roof. The walkway was lined with pink and white roses. The cottage sparkled in the southern California sunshine while being bathed in the warm ocean wind. The house was within walking distance of the beach and Karrie could hear the seagulls welcoming her to her new home as she rolled down the car window and looked upon the their house for the first time. Mr. Wilson walked out to the garage to greet them. He gallantly walked over to Mrs. Wilson's side door and opened her door to help her out of the car. He gently kissed his wife on the side of the cheek which made Karrie's heart flutter at his kindness and manners.

"So, is this our new guest?" Mr. Wilson smiled down at Karrie who was still fumbling with her seat belt trying to get out of the car.

"It's not as complicated as you are making it, dear," Mrs. Wilson quietly said to Karrie. "Pull up the latch and the seat belt will open."

That was the first time Karrie felt she had disappointed Mrs. Wilson, and she would come to learn it would be the beginning of many more disappointments. Karrie would never be neat enough or smart enough for Mrs. Wilson. Karrie talked too much when they had company, or she didn't talk enough when the Wilsons' family members came to visit. But the greatest annoyance Karrie would feel from Mrs. Wilson was her disdain for Karrie's faith.

"It doesn't bother me that she's a Christian," Mrs. Wilson would tell her friends and relatives, "it's just that she's not the reasonable go-to-church-once-in-while type of Christian but the fanatical Bible quoting type of Christian."

Then Mrs. Wilson would wrinkle up her nose and say, "she's clearly been deluded by religious zeal. Not like the 'Marxian opiate of the people' kind." Mrs. Wilson would smirk as she would lean in and whisper, "More like a 'desperate soul reaching out for mind numbing heroin' kind."

This remark would inspire hushed laughter from Mrs. Wilson's friends. Mrs. Wilson would never say this in Karrie's presence, but it was always within earshot, and Karrie could still hear her and the echo of the polite laughter down the hall from the living room. Karrie knew she was on display and clearly not measuring up to the expectations of the adults around her. Yet all those disappointments wouldn't happen until many months of staying with the Wilsons.

The day that Karrie arrived at the Wilsons' house, they seemed to be the perfect family who would fulfill Karrie's deepest hope that she would be valued and loved as she had always wished. That afternoon Karrie had walked into a country cottage with a real overstuffed couch and a Persian rug. The dining room was filled with pink and white balloons and the dining room table was dressed in a lacy tablecloth with a white cake surrounded by meat and cheese platers. A sparkly banner was draped across the living room's light fixture that read, "Welcome Home, Karrie!"

Mr. Wilson carried Karrie's things into her new room while Karrie sat down at the dining table amongst nervous laughter and joined her new family for a light summer dinner. After dinner the family took a walk to watch the sunset over the ocean. Standing in the halo of orange sunlight between the Wilsons, Karrie's heart almost burst with gratitude at the anticipation of a new home. That evening as Karrie snuggled beneath a warm yellow rose comforter, she drifted to sleep as her body relaxed in the hope of a greater security and stability of domestic perfection.

But her dreams of domestic perfection would not come into fruition. Instead from Karrie's perspective, this dream seemed to turn into hard, cheapened plastic.

After Karrie had been with the Wilsons for about a month, she started to feel the hardness of the plastic one Saturday morning. She was cleaning her room, trying to finish it up by noon so she could get to church to attend a youth group carwash they were holding to raise money for camp.

Mrs. Wilson knocked impatiently at Karrie's door, and pushed open the door while Karrie was on her hands and knees trying to clean under the bed.

"Karrie," Mrs. Wilson impatiently whispered, "what is this?"

Karrie sat up and look questioningly at Mrs. Wilson.

"It's a towel," Karrie said.

"Yes, dear, I know it is towel," Mrs. Wilson said through tightened lips. "But it has not been treated like a towel. As you may have noticed, it has been treated like a rag, and it has been wadded up and thrown in the corner of our linen closet."

"I folded it like you showed me." Karrie's voice began to tremble.

"No, dear, you did not. I know you *think* you did. But you did not. Now let's go over this again. Stand up and take the towel in your hands."

"I am a little scared I will be late for church."

"Church will wait," Mrs. Wilson slowly said. "There are more important things at stake here than your fabled, precious religion." Mrs. Wilson closed her eyes and shook her head as if she was trying to dismiss a thought. "That's not what I meant. Of course, your faith is important, but have you ever heard the idea of being so heavenly minded that you are no earthly good? Well, I am going to teach you some earthly goodness this morning and then you can go bathe in your heavenly idealism."

She tossed the towel to Karrie.

"Okay, let's go over this again. These are the instructions that we have in this household for folding towels. First, you place the towel on a flat surface."

Karrie spread out the towel on her bed.

"No, Karrie, not your bed! It will wrinkle there!"

Karrie moved the towel to the floor.

"No! Not on the dirty floor," Mrs. Wilson snapped.

"Then, where? I don't have a flat surface in here."

Mrs. Wilson rolled eyes and then whispered, "Take out the upper shelf in the closet It is removable dear. And lay the towel across the board and use that as your flat surface."

Karrie reached up and took out the shelf and followed the instructions that Miss Wilson gave to her in a threatening whisper.

"Now fold the towel in half by placing the corners of the towel neatly perfectly matching the corners, then fold your towel over by matching the corners from the left side to the right. Fold the corners over again from the left to then fold it into thirds."

With trembling hands, Karrie followed her instructions perfectly and then handed the towel back to Mrs. Wilson.

"Very good," said Miss Wilson through her tightened smile. "Now let's try it with a larger bath towel."

"But my church car wash!" Karrie protested.

"It will keep." Mrs. Wilson smiled her perfect smile. "I will make sure you get to the car wash on time, I promise. Now take the other towel and let's try this together."

Mrs. Wilson handed Karrie another towel and Karrie complied.

Karrie never knew why Mrs. Wilson would get angry at the littlest of things, but she understood that her job at the restaurant was a great point of irritation for Mrs. Wilson.

The morning Karrie told the Wilsons she wanted to take a job at the restaurant where she and Lo'laini had won the culinary contest, Mrs. Wilson told Karrie she didn't want to talk about it then. The Wilsons' college-aged son, Alex, had just returned home for a week. He had been away studying in New York when Karrie first arrived and returned home while Karrie was at work. There were preparations to be made for family outings and cleaning out Alex's room, so Mrs. Wilson told Karrie that perhaps she would discuss with her after dinner. Karrie was frightened Mrs. Wilson would say no to her new job and that she would lose touch with Lo'laini, so she called her social worker. Her social worker said she would call Mrs. Wilson to discuss it with her that afternoon.

When Karrie walked into the house after school, she knew she had been discussed among the three adults during the day.

Alex had introduced himself to her awkwardly over dinner and offered to help Karrie with her homework because he knew she was having trouble in school. But the air was already thick with the conflict over Karrie's job and Karrie's apparent betrayal by calling her social worker instead of waiting to talk to Mrs. Wilson that evening.

~~

Mrs. Wilson's unexpected call from Karrie's social worker had surprised her with the new revelations that Karrie might be leaving their family to be reunited with her mother. The conversation was still ringing in Mrs. Wilson's ears . . .

"Karrie called me this afternoon and told me she was concerned you weren't going to let her take a summer job. I was hoping we could do some interfacing a little bit about this issue. I am concerned that you are not allowing Karrie to make her choices about work and extra curricular activity."

"I am not standing in the way of Karrie's choice!" Mrs. Wilson protested, "I didn't even know about this job until this morning and I am shocked. It is just that Karrie and I had previous plans, she told me that she wanted to take ballet lessons and I already paid for lessons."

"Well, you know, Dianne, I appreciate that you are feeling a little betrayed by Karrie's indecision here, but you know she is thinking of leaving to be reunited with her mother and maybe she is just trying to create a little emotional distance between the two of you to make her departure easier."

"Leaving? No! No one told me she was leaving to be reunited with her mother!" Mrs. Wilson's voice began to rise.

"I am sorry, Mrs. Wilson . . . Karrie was supposed to tell you this."

"How is that safe? How is it possible for her to be reunited with that woman?" Mrs. Wilson stammered trying to hold back her indignation.

"You knew this was one of the options for Karrie when you took her into your home, Mrs. Wilson."

"Well, we are going to talk this afternoon and I'll get this straightened out," Mrs. Wilson snapped back in a business-like tone.

"No, I am sorry Mrs. Wilson." The social worker sighed and put her hand over her eyes to soothe a splitting headache that had been tormenting her all week. "I am going to ask you to wait until all three of us talk. I know you are upset, and this is a delicate issue for Karrie. Can I come by Friday and we'll all talk?"

"Yes," Mrs. Wilson's soft voice returned. "Come by Friday, by all means. I will take a short day at work and you can come by at three pm."

~~

After a tortuously quiet dinner, Karrie retreated to her room, only to hear Mr. and Mrs. Wilson argue while they cleaned up the dining room table.

"She doesn't need to work! And there are other things for her to do! Better things! Things I can help her with!"

The dishes clashed in the background as Mrs. Wilson complained.

"Quiet, she'll hear you." Mr. Wilson's warm voice tried to calm the brewing storm.

"I won't be quiet. I don't care if she hears me! How do you think I felt getting that call at work today? How long do you think she knew about this ridiculous plan? Her mother? She was filthy when she came here. She knew nothing about basic hygiene! I am not going to passively turn that child back over to that woman!"

"Dianne, it's not your choice, you know that."

"So, I just have to watch it, watch the girl's life go down the drain with that trash. I know what it is like to be in a house like her mother's. I can give her opportunities, opportunities she won't have if she leaves this house!"

Mr. Wilson sat down next to his wife. "You heard the social worker. Working gives Karrie a sense of self-esteem, and a little bit of power, and some spending cash."

"I can give her spending cash, but she won't take it from me because I am the bad guy. I am the enemy! This house has schedules," she continued. "Who is supposed to take her to work and pick her up from work?"

"The same person who was going to take her to ballet lessons," Mr. Wilson said.

"No, no, no, no, I am not going there with you." Mrs. Wilson got up and went back to the kitchen. "I was always chauffeur when Alex was growing up and I didn't mind it, because I know that is what women do, we make the homes, we make everything pretty. I didn't mind doing it with Karrie for ballet lessons or tutoring because those were things that would benefit her, but not for a waitressing job, not even a waitress job—the job of a busboy!"

"Then I will take her," said Mr. Wilson.

"No, you won't," Mrs. Wilson barked back. "You always make yourself the good guy in these situations. She'll take the bus. I won't have you covering this up with some gesture you think is kind. If she wants to work as a waitress, she can live like one. She'll take the bus. That's what waitresses do!!"

"Knock, knock, anyone there." Karrie heard the voice of Alex outside her door.

"Yeah," said Karrie. "Come in."

"Dominos?" Alex held up a pale beige wooden box.

"Okay." Karrie sat up in her bed and wiped away a few tears.

Alex lay his tall limber body across the bed. He laid out a game board and placed the dominos face down. "Okay. We each take eight pieces and no cheating; do you hear me?" He pointed his finger at Karrie, and she smiled.

There was a moment of silence while they each looked at their pieces. Then Alex placed a domino in the middle of the board.

"Don't take them too seriously. I mean the fight out there. Believe me it has nothing to do with you."

"Oh yeah? They seem to be saying my name a lot. They don't seem to like me very much." Karrie placed the next matching domino on the board.

"That's what I mean about not taking it too seriously." Alex studied the board then placed a domino that crossed Karrie's last play. "I was a little worried when they said they had decided to take in a foster daughter. It felt like they were trying to fix something with a new kid because I was leaving for college. I also knew there was a lot of stuff going on with Mom that was going to come out with a new kid around here."

Karrie connected one of her dominos to Alex's. "What were they trying to fix?"

"My grandma died. She had been sick for a long time and Mom used to take care of her. So, I don't know how to say this but . . . " Alex's eyes scanned the board to find a place for his next domino, then placed one at the end of Karrie's last domino. "My grandma was a good grandma, but she was not a good mother. Mom and Dad would never talk about it, they never had to. You could see it by the way she kept house and talked to Mom. She talked to her in ways she would never talk to me. At family gatherings you could cut the tension between Grandma and Mom with a knife when they were in the room together. I don't why Mom felt she had to take care of Grandma. We could've easily afforded a nurse, but you know, who can figure anyone out? Hey Squirt, it's your turn."

Alex smiled at Karrie the same way her brother used to smile at her. Karrie searched for another domino.

"So, Mom kind of fell apart when Grandma died. I came home and found her bent over some old baby pictures crying. Mom doesn't cry easily. 'She never could love me,' Mom sobbed. I sat next to her and held her hand. 'I know,' I said. I regretted saying that the moment the words came out of me. Mom looked at me as if I stabbed her. I was telling her I knew the secret she had worked so hard to conceal. I had to leave for college that fall, so I was the one who brought up family therapy before I left, and they agreed. We all went to family therapy for a while."

"I go to therapy." Karrie looked up and smiled and placed another domino on the board.

"You like it?" asked Alex.

"Sometimes. Yeah . . . sometimes," Karrie said.

"Sometimes here, too." Alex crossed Karrie's domino. "In therapy I found out Mom and Dad didn't have any rules in their homes growing up. You know, beds were never made and dishes stayed in the sink for weeks. It was hard for them to live like this, and it hurt them. So, when I was growing up, they made all these rules. Not that I minded them, but it was their way of keeping me safe. So, you know the towel thing, and the making the perfect bed thing?"

Karrie looked up, nodded, and smiled at Alex.

"She's just trying to keep you safe. I know it doesn't make a lot of sense," Alex said as he shrugged his shoulders, "but I think Mom's trying to get something back, something she's lost, with you being here. It's so obvious she can't do it. I think she thinks by fixing you, she can fix herself." Alex looked at his dominos and threw his hands in the air. "I don't have a matching domino. I guess you get to finish the game."

Karrie placed her last domino on the board.

"You win, kid." Alex started to fold the board.

"No wait! Don't fold it up yet. I want to take a picture of the board with my phone," Karrie said while reaching over to the side of her bed to pull out her phone.

"Why?" Alex asked.

"Because it looks like a staircase." Karrie aimed her phone at the board and pressed the button to take a picture.

Alex looked at Karrie's picture and shrugged his shoulders. "No, it looks like a spider web." He laughed.

As he got up to leave the room Karrie asked, "One question? Was your grandma a Christian? I mean was she religious?"

"Yeah totally religious but also totally a closed book. I wish I knew her better. I love my mom. And I loved my grandma, but there was real pain between those two."

Alex turned to walk toward the door and then turned back around and looked at Karrie. "Listen I know you're thinking about going home to be with your mom."

"Yeah, your mom seemed really angry about that. I hate that I keep making adults angry at me." Karrie looked down at her hand, a little embarrassed to look at Alex's face.

"No, she's not angry. She's worried. Don't sell her too short. She is worried about what might happen to you while she's still remembering what happened to her. I know she's making some mistakes here, but she is trying. Like all people do, trying but failing. So, what are you going to do?" Alex asked.

"I don't know."

"I just want you to know, in spite of those angry voices out there, you are loved here, and we want what is best for you. Does it feel like home to you here?"

Karrie looked up from her hands. "No," she said right before Alex opened the door and left the room.

The heavy moan of the bus pulling to side of the curb brought Karrie back from her musings of the events of the last week. The bus rolled to a stop about three blocks from Karrie's house. Mr. Wilson was waiting at the bus stop, holding a cup of hot chocolate and a flashlight.

"So, how's the young professional woman?" asked Mr. Wilson as Karrie got off the bus.

"Tired." Karrie took the hot chocolate from Mr. Wilson. He shone the flashlight before them as they started on their walk home.

"Hey look." Mr. Wilson smiled as they turned to walk toward the house, "The fog is clearing up."

Chapter 17

Monday morning, Karrie found herself back at the courthouse staring at the same familiar white plastic chairs.

"Hi, stranger." Karrie heard Miss Ellen's voice from behind her. She gasped and turned around leaning into the familiar soft arms.

"Thank you for coming." Karrie smiled and stepped back, looking up at Miss Ellen.

"Thank you for asking me to be your advocate." Miss Ellen placed her arm around Karrie to give her a sideways squeeze.

"I didn't know who to ask. They asked me if I wanted an advocate, and I thought of you. You know Miss Sophia doesn't work there anymore. Her fiancé died. Did you know?"

"I heard that." Miss Ellen brushed a rouge hair out of Karrie's eyes. "She's a strong girl, she'll get through it."

"What is an advocate supposed to do anyway?"

"I'm supposed be here and sit beside you and make you feel comfortable." Miss Ellen started to sit down in one of white chairs behind them. Karrie stopped her.

"Then walk me away from those ugly white chairs." Karrie grabbed one of Ellen's arms and pulled her away.

Miss Ellen laughed, and they both walked toward the window across from the chairs.

"So what should I do?" Karrie questioningly at Miss Ellen.

"You should talk to the judge," Miss Ellen smiled back at Karrie.

"I know that. I mean, about Mom—what I should do?"

Miss Ellen looked blankly back at Karrie.

"Oh," said Karrie, "is this one of those situations where you are supposed be impartial?"

Miss Ellen nodded.

"I hate impartial."

"Excuse me." Miss Ellen and Karrie turned away from the window and saw a tall police officer with a clipboard in his hand. "The judge will see you now," he said.

Miss Ellen and Karrie walked into a wood-paneled room that had walls lined with large bookcases full of dictionary-sized blue, black, and gray books neatly arranged by size and color. A middle-aged woman was seated in a black leather chair behind a large, perfectly polished desk. There were two smaller leather chairs across from her and one in the center of the room. In one corner of the room, there was a woman who was typing on a small machine; in the other corner, there was a camera. A man in a dark pin-striped suit sat on the side of the desk with a small laptop he balanced on his knees. He had slicked-back hair, and Karrie thought he sat as if he were posing for a fashion magazine. She also thought he gave her a look as if she were a three-year-old.

Miss Ellen and Karrie took their seats in the chairs across from the judge.

"Okay, Karrie, we're having this meeting in my office. My office is called the judge's chambers. This meeting is not going to be like the other meeting we had in the front courtroom a few months ago when your dad was on trial. No one is on trial here. This is just between you and me. In this meeting, we are going to try to establish whether we need to have another meeting in the courtroom about the living conditions in your previous home."

The middle-aged woman looked over her reading glasses at Karrie. Her words were soft and clear and put Karrie at ease.

"When you said, 'previous home,' you meant my mom's house, right?" said Karrie.

"Yes, Karrie, your mom's house," said the judge.

"But there are other people here," Karrie nodded toward the man on one side of the desk and then at the woman who was quietly typing in the other the corner. "You said this meeting was just between you and me, so why are these other people here?"

"This lady is Sharron. She is the courtroom stenographer. She is writing down what we are saying so there is no confusion as to what was said." The judge gestured across her desk at the fashionable young man. "The man is Mr. Null. He is your father's lawyer."

"Why is my father's lawyer here?" asked Karrie.

"Because your father loves you very much and still wants to be a part of your life," said Mr. Null.

"Counselor," said the judge, throwing Mr. Null an irritated glance, "I don't want to warn you again! You are here solely as an observer and may not address this child. You know the rules." The judge turned back to Karrie. "I think you know your father is filing an appeal on his conviction."

"So my dad will know what I am saying?" A knot arose in Karrie's stomach as she looked at the camera on the other side of the room.

"Not directly, Karrie," said the judge. "That camera is there to record our conversation, so we make sure exactly what was said in this meeting. We will also compare the audio of the video with the notes Sharron is taking, to make sure everything is accurate, and nothing has been missed. Mr. Null is here to make sure you are not going to be unduly influenced by any of the adults in this room. He knows that he may stay if he agrees to act according to the terms I have set for him."

The judge glanced once more at Mr. Null, and then Karrie went on to say, "But the conversation is not really between you and me. Other people can see this video and read these notes, can't they?"

"Not necessarily. I will write an opinion taken from these notes and tapes. The lawyers will read my opinion. Your father will not hear your words directly."

"But he'll know what I said." Karrie looked somberly back at the ground.

"Karrie, part of my job is to keep you safe, and I take my job very seriously. When you meet with your counselor or social workers, those meetings are confidential, so your parents have no right to know about what goes on there. But this meeting is a legal meeting about custody and visitation. Your parents still have those rights that I must respect."

"So you're like the boss of the trial?" asked Karrie.

"Again, it's not a trial, Karrie. It is conversation, and the law is the boss of this conversation. I make sure it is enforced." The judge took off her glasses and rubbed her eyes; then she sighed and said, "Unfortunately, or fortunately, the people of California still believe that in most cases, a child's interest is best served when the child is in the care of their biological parents. So your parents' rights are considered in this room as well."

"So you can't really keep me safe." Karrie rose from her chair and walked toward the bookcase and looked up and down at the books. "Have you read all these books?" she asked as she passed her finger over the sides of the books.

"I have read some of those books." The judge smiled. "Most of the books, I use to look things up I need when considering a case."

"I love books," Karrie whispered quietly.

"Maybe one day you'll have as many books as I have."

"I don't think so. I have problems reading and spelling, but I hope so," said Karrie as she sat down again in her chair.

"I hope you will, too," said the judge. "Now, Karrie, I've heard you have a new job that came about because you won a contest for a recipe you created."

"No, it was Lo'laini's mother's recipe. I wrote the proposal, and Lo'laini provided the recipe," Karrie explained.

"And you showed initiative when you entered the contest. Is Lo'laini a good friend of yours?"

"She's my best friend. I met her in the group home. She's a better cook than I am, but I get along with people better than she does, so we make a great team. We're bussing tables for the catered events this summer at the La Jolla restaurant. If we work out, Mr. Rodriguez says we can work during the school year, too."

"How are things with your foster parents, the Wilsons?"

"They're okay, I guess. I have a great room, but most of the time, they don't bother me, and I don't bother them."

"So, it is not ideal," said the judge.

"It's not home," said Karrie as she remembered her conversation with Lo'laini.

"Now let's talk about your brothers. According to my notes, Pete just turned eighteen, and he is the eldest. He has chosen to go into the military rather than serve time in a detention center for boys after he got into a fight in his foster home and . . . " The judge paused as she turned the page. A look of surprise came over her face. "Andrew's foster parents are seeking to adopt him."

"He doesn't want to go to counseling with me and Mom," said Karrie, looking down at her hands. "I don't know why."

"Your Honor, I would really like you to address some of the concerns my client and I have given you in writing about Karrie's emotional health," said Mr. Null.

"My emotional health!" Karrie said, raising one eyebrow and standing up from her seat. "My dad is concerned about my emotional health after what he did to me?"

"Karrie, sit down. Don't let him get you angry," the judge said.

"Counselor, this is neither a trial, nor an investigation into this ward's emotional health," the judge said sternly. "We are assessing whether or not this child is to be returned to the home of her mother. The questions you have may or may not be relevant to this case. And I will not let you divert this meeting for any other cause than the one that has already been specified!"

"Can we at least address her nightmares and when they began?" Mr. Null asked in an annoyed tone. "I think her perception of reality is relevant as to what she experienced or what she has simply dreamed up."

Karrie felt a stab of betrayal by the lawyer's question. "You know about my nightmares?"

"Mr. Null, do you care to explain yourself," the judge asked.

The judge's sharp tone unnerved the well-dressed young lawyer. He backed off and took his seat again.

He looks like a school yard bully who has just gotten into trouble, Karrie thought as she saw him feigning confidence by sticking out his jaw and shrugging his shoulders. He stammered, "I would refer Your Honor to the therapist report to the court."

"The therapist report," Karrie gasped, fighting back tears.

The judge rolled her eyes and turned to Karrie. "Karrie, Mr. Null knows nothing about your nightmares. Your therapist gave us an assessment, which means she filled out a very basic form about your well-being. In that form, she said she believed you had symptoms of post-traumatic stress disorder from your abuse. Nightmares are a common symptom of PTSD. Your therapist did not betray any of your confidences. Mr. Null is playing what is called a lawyer's trick, and because he has played such a trick, he has a lost the right to remain in this meeting."

"Your Honor, I must really protest," Mr. Null started to say, stammering.

"File it with the court, Counselor!" the judge snapped back at him.

Mr. Null turned red. He was shaking as he picked up his laptop and walked toward the door. The stenographer looked up at Mr. Null with laughing eyes as he shut the door behind him, and Miss Ellen squeezed Karrie's hand.

The moment Mr. Null brought up the word *nightmare*, it had taken her to a different place. Her nightmares had haunted her for years. Always, just when she was beginning to feel safe again, a nightmare would return. Her father was never present in any of her dreams, but his soured-wine breath and the smell of his dirty clothes was always there. The dreams were nothing extraordinary: she would be walking to school or playing with her friends, and then she would hear her father's breathing and realize there was no place to run or hide. For the rest of the dream, she would be struggling to wake up.

The dream that haunted her most was the one she had about the group home. In this dream, she would be coming home from the school. She would open the door to the room she shared with Lo'laini, where she could smell the lilac-scented sheets Miss Sophia had washed. When she pulled back the sheets, all she could smell was her father. Then her bedsheets would start to bleed. The dreams did not simply haunt her at night. There were times during the day when the memory of her father would flood her mind, and she could not get the vision of his abuse out of her thoughts. Once, when her boyfriend Tom tried to kiss her at church camp, her father's smell flashed through her mind, and she pushed him away. At that moment, she thought he would dump her and never call her again. He didn't, but she could never explain to him what was going on inside of her when she didn't want him to touch her.

Now she sat in this wood-paneled room full of books, with these two ladies in business suits, and she was supposed to just talk about it here, in a place where it would be recorded for everyone to gawk at?

"Karrie," the judge said softly, "I know it is hard to come back from that scene we just had, but I promise you, we are not going to talk about anything as intimate as your nightmares. And your father will not be told any information, either, on that subject from this interview. Now, I would like to talk to you about your mother's house. I will be interviewing her in about five minutes, and I need some idea as to how you felt while you were living there and how you feel about returning there now."

"I loved my home, and I hated my home," Karrie said quietly. "I loved the canyon and the smell of my grandmother's garden, and that I could walk to church on Sunday and wouldn't have to call anyone for a ride. I loved walking with Mom down to North Park to shop at local stores and our walks to the laundromat. I loved talking to her on those walks. I loved taking the bus to Horton Plaza to see a movie, but I hated . . . " Karrie's voice tapered off, and round, hot tears began to roll down her cheeks. "I hated that our house smelled like yesterday's garbage and that there was dog poop on our living room floor. I hated the smell of dirty dishes, the roaches, and the constant clutter of dirty clothes on the floor. I hated the embarrassment I felt when I found out neighbors called our house the "garbage heap." And I hated my dad's . . . his visits."

Karrie swallowed hard as tears began to roll uncontrollably down her cheeks. "I hated his breath, his touch, and feeling his weight on top of me." She sobbed. She wiped her tears away and looked directly at the judge. "I loved it because it was home, but I also hated that place because of what happened to me there. I have also never felt at home anyplace since I've left that house, though."

The judge put her hand on Karrie's trembling hands. The room was quiet.

Chapter 18

"So, Karrie," the judge said quietly while holding her hand, "are you ready? Are you ready to tell your mother some of the things you said to me?"

"I want to see my mom," Karrie said, "but I don't think I can say the same things I said to you to her."

"What do you think you can say to her, Karrie?"

"That I want to come home, but"—Karrie paused and took a deep breath—"I don't want to see Dad."

"Well, that's a start. Let's start the conversation and see where it goes." The judge nodded at the bailiff who was standing by the door. The bailiff exited the room.

Karrie could hear him call out to her mother. "Mrs. Leary, you may come in now."

Mama tentatively walked from the room where she had been watching the clock and stood in the frame of the front door. She smiled at Karrie. All of Karrie's life, when Mama had smiled at her in that way, Karrie would run and be caught up into her mother's arms. Karrie wanted to run this time, too. She wanted to laugh and feel her mother's warm embrace. But her feet held her to the ground. She didn't know why. Karrie looked at Mama and smiled, but she could not run to her.

Mama's hurt look at her refusal burned a hole in Karrie's heart as her feet remained steadfast on the ground.

"Mrs. Leary." The judge stood and extended her hand for Mama to shake.

Mama entered the room and took the judge's hand. The judge pointed to a chair, and Mama took her seat.

"Cute haircut," Mama said to the stenographer, who looked up and smiled at her. "It would be better with some highlights right around your face. It'll lighten up your complexion. Come into my shop, we got a deal on for this week."

The stenographer looked nervously at the judge.

"Am I allowed to say things like that here?" Mama asked.

"There would be a strong conflict of interests for us to visit your shop, Mrs. Leary." The judge smiled at Mama to put her at ease. "You work at Mission Valley, don't you?"

"Yes, I've been working there for nine years now. We remodeled last year. You'd be surprised what a splash of color and lighting will do."

"Yes," said the judge, looking sideways at the mirror on her desk. "I think I could stand a little color myself next time I get my hair done."

Mama started to say something, but the judge stopped her. "No special offers," she said and she smiled. "I can see you are a constant professional."

The judge's last comment was followed by some nervous laughter from everyone in the room. Karrie felt a strong sense of pride swelling inside her at her mother's expertise.

"You have something to say to your daughter, don't you, Mrs. Leary?" asked the judge.

Mama forced a smile and leaned in from her chair toward Karrie, who was sitting across from her. "I miss you, little girl." Mama's voice trembled as she spoke. "I know there were things I should've known about, but I didn't. I want you to come home again. I've lost the boys, and I don't want to lose you, too—"

"I want to come home again, too!" Karrie interrupted, and Mama reached out to grasp Karrie's hand.

"It's good that we both agree on that point. Now I've been lookin' for an apartment, and I found something. It is closer to your school. It's near Balboa

Park, and I know how much you love that place." Mama started to pull out some photos.

"What about our old house?" Karrie asked.

Mama closed her eyes as if she was trying to hold back a wave of emotion. "We don't have that house anymore, little girl. It takes two incomes to pay the mortgage, and now your daddy's income is gone. He's going to be gone for a long time before he comes home again, and this is all I can afford on my own income."

"What do you mean 'before he comes back?'" Karrie pulled her hands away from her mother.

"It's going to be ten years or more, and you'll be long gone by the time he comes back, so you won't have anything to worry about," Mama said.

"Karrie, how do you feel about what your mother just said?" asked the judge.

"I already know what she feels about it," Mama blurted out at the judge. She closed her eyes again to try to calm herself. "You know, Your Honor, this can't just be all about her feelings."

"Tell me what you mean by that," the judge prompted.

Mama stood up and walked toward the window. She waited for a moment, and then she took a deep breath. "You got to understand something here, Your Honor." She took another deep breath. "I'm a success story. I'm the first in my family to attend a junior college and get a professional license. I'm the first business owner in my family, even though the bank still owns most of my shop. And I was the first to buy"—Mama's voice shook with tears—"a house. Now I've lost most of that. What I have left is, at best, in jeopardy. I don't have my house or my boys, and I'm just hanging on to my business. I don't want to blame Karrie for speaking up. But I'd give my life to turn the clock back six months or so."

"The problem with your reply," the judge said somberly "is that the world you want to turn the clock back to restore was a world that tortured your daughter."

"I know," Mama whispered. She walked back to the chair where she had been sitting. She lifted her chin so she could look into Karrie's eyes. "I know he hurt you, little girl," she whispered. "I know that hurt you real bad, and you don't ever have to be alone with him again. I'll obey whatever rules they give me on that account. I didn't protect you, and I know I should have. Maybe because I wasn't protected when I was a little girl, but I keep feeling if I turned out all right . . . "

"It's not a matter of you 'turning out all right,'" interjected the judge. "The point is that what happened to your daughter, and possibly to you, is illegal. You have to come to an understanding of that fact, or we can't move forward."

"I'm trying to understand that," Mama said to the judge without looking up from the ground. And then she looked back at her daughter. "So I guess it's going to take some learning on my part, Kar. But you need to understand my life has changed in a way that can't be repaired. I've lost so much, and I don't want to lose my husband. I can't divorce him, girl. You don't ever need to see him again, but I can't divorce him. You will be grown and gone before he returns, ya know."

Karrie nodded and leaned into her mother's embrace.

"Well," said the judge, "we don't have a perfect situation here, but I think we have a workable situation, and if you continue with counseling, both of you can begin remediation and then move on to reconciliation."

Chapter 19

After six months of counseling and planning a future with her mom, the thought of moving out of the Wilsons' house felt like a relief to Karrie. She began to pack things up two months before her move. The thought of moving home was both exciting and frightening. Josh and Tom said they'd help with the move, and Pastor Mike helped out with his truck. Lo'laini said she would supervise.

"Josh," Tom struggled to say, hanging on to the twin sized mattress stuck in the apartment door, "turn the mattress more to the other side. Then maybe we can squeeze it through the door."

"Please don't scrape the paint on the doorframe," said Mama. "I want to get my deposit back when I leave this place."

"Don't worry, Mrs. Leary," laughed Lo'laini from the dining room. "These boys aren't all brawn. They're the picture of grace, too."

"We're ignoring comments from the peanut gallery," Josh said as he guided the mattress safely through the door. The room erupted into enthusiastic applause by Karrie, Mama, and Lo'laini as Josh and Tom carried the mattress to Karrie's room and placed it on her bedframe.

"Wow," said Josh as he looked at the bed. "You girls put this together by yourselves?"

"She's beautiful, and she can use a screwdriver, too," said Lo'laini, waving her tool kit in the air.

"So, Karrie, how does it feel?" Tom asked, looking around the room.

"It almost feels like my room. I've put all my clothes away, but my pictures and books are still in boxes. As soon as I am fully unpacked, I think I can call it home."

"Well, I've got to catch the bus to get to work before my shift starts," said Mama, standing at the door. "It's good to have you home, baby." She hugged Karrie and kissed her on the cheek, and then walked out the door.

"So what's the plan?" asked Lo'laini, looking at Josh and Tom after Mama left.

"Well, if you girls think you have the stamina for a strenuous bike ride," said Josh, looking at Lo'laini, "we were thinking about having lunch at Balboa Park. But I wouldn't want you to strain yourself and make you break a nail or anything."

Lo'laini got a gleam in her eye. "You're calling a mile ride to Balboa Park hard?" She pushed Josh out of her way and started to walk briskly toward her bike that was chained to a nearby fence on the side of the apartment. "You might want to stay out of my way. I'd hate to run you over on El Cajon Boulevard." Lo'laini looked over her should as she mounted her bike. As she started to ride away, she shouted at Tom, Karrie, and Josh, "You know what they say—it is hard to soar with eagles when tied to the ground with turkeys!"

Josh got on his bike and began to ride after Lo'laini. Tom waited for Karrie to finish locking the front the door, and then they started on their bikes in hot pursuit of Josh and Lo'laini. Soon they had caught up with Josh and Lo'laini. The two boys wove in and out between the two girls, taunting them as they peddled down El Cajon Boulevard and turned onto Park Avenue toward Balboa Park. When the girls turned into the park in front of the Natural History Museum, the boys were nowhere to be found.

"Where'd they go?" asked Karrie, looking around.

"Look on the other side of the fountain," Lo'laini said, nodding her head forward.

Josh was laying by the fountain as if he was sound asleep, and Tom was pointing at his watch. He smiled at Lo'laini and Karrie as they rode over to the fountain.

"I hope you didn't tire yourself out by that long ride." Josh yawned and opened one eye looking at Karrie and Lo'laini as they stopped their bikes by the fountain.

"Don't worry about me." Lo'laini dismounted her bike and sat down beside the fountain.

"But you seem all out of breath." Tom stood up to hold Karrie's bike while she dismounted.

"Well, seems to me we were promised something to eat." Karrie looked up at Tom.

"Okay, I'll get it. Me, man, me go hunt for food." Tom hunched over, imitating a caveman.

"Big hunter men find food for weak, frail women." Josh jokingly copied Tom beating his chest.

"Watch it," Lo'laini warned, pointing at Josh.

"We women find place to eat while men get food." Karrie pulled Lo'laini up from her seat by the fountain.

"Why are you pulling me up?" Lo'laini pulled away to sit down again. "Me princess. I sit around and look pretty."

"We'll be in front of the Casa del Prado by the big tree," Karrie called out to Josh as she grabbed her bike and pulled Lo'laini, dragging her across the park.

Tom turned around and started walking across the park toward a concession stand.

Karrie waited until Tom was out of hearing range before she poked Lo'laini and said, "So, you and Josh sure seem chummy."

"What can I do?" Lo'laini shrugged her shoulders. "I can't get the boy to leave me alone. It's an act of mercy, really. Someone has to socialize with the boy. He really is helpless without me."

"Do you ever hear from Kevin anymore?" asked Karrie as they came to a tree in front of Casa del Prado.

"Sometimes. But he knows by now that I'm not coming back to the islands, just like I know it now."

"I'm sorry," Karrie said as she handed her bike to Lo'laini, who walked their bikes over to the bike rack to lock them up.

Karrie took a flowered shawl out of her backpack and laid it on the lawn. Lo'laini returned and sat on the shawl. She pulled out her phone to show Karrie a picture of Kevin. "He just sent this to me. Things are okay between me and him. I think we both just realize things don't always happen like we expect them to, and sometimes that's okay. I am still really glad he was there for me when my mom died."

Just then, they saw a juggler pass by on a unicycle. Behind him, a cluster of children gathered around. The blue and red balls passed in rapid succession in a circle above his head, and then they flew up and down and from side to side. Then behind the juggler, Karrie saw something else being thrown in the air.

"That is sooo embarrassing. I can't even stand to look!" groaned Lo'laini, "That boy tries way too hard sometimes."

"Lo'laini, that's not what I think it is, is it?" asked Karrie.

Behind the juggler, Tom was juggling four hero sandwiches, and Josh was following him, shaking his head, carrying four large paper cups. When Karrie saw Tom juggling the sandwiches, she squealed in delight. "Bravo!" she shouted as Tom approached them.

Lo'laini simply rolled her eyes.

"For my ladies," Tom said with an eloquent bow.

"For anyone who wants them," Josh said, placing the drinks in the middle of the group.

Lo'laini looked up to the sky and prayed, "Thank You, God, for good food."

After the papers were ravishingly torn off the hot sandwiches, the group began eating and laughing. They laughed at the juggler and his corny style of throwing the balls in the air, to the amazement of the children who gathered around him watching. They laughed because they remembered they had been those children just a few years ago. They moaned about school beginning and wondered if the next grade would be harder than this one. They wondered at the symmetry of the towering tree in front of them whose roots seemed to be a reflection of its branches.

Lo'laini researched the tree in front of Casa Del Prado on her phone and found it was called the Moreton Bay Fig, and it was a hundred years old. Then they found themselves wondering how many people had talked about the tree before them and how many would ask the same questions after them. They talked about who the cool kids were at school and at church and why some kids were deemed cool and other kids were not. The talked about the places they would travel to, the jobs they were going to have, and the homes they would one day build. Soon all the conversation was quieted, and all the food was gone.

Lo'laini lay back on the grass and put her feet on the small of Josh's back, who was lying on his stomach at the bottom of the shawl. Karrie leaned up against the palm tree next to Tom. He quietly slipped a bracelet onto her wrist made of baby's breath and grass he had hand-knotted together during the conversation.

"Hey, Karrie." Josh threw a small blade of grass, tickling Karrie's face, to get her attention. "Have you figured out what you're going to say in your testimony at the beginning of the month?"

"No." Karrie yawned. "I mean, I know it is going to be something about why I believe in Jesus, but beyond that, I haven't figured it out."

"Well, I think he chose the right person." Tom sat up, brushing himself off. "Karrie's the toughest person I know."

"Not that tough." Karrie looked over at Lo'laini.

"I don't know anyone else that lived away from their mom at our age," Tom said, looking up at Karrie.

"Maybe that's what you should talk about during your testimony?"

Lo'laini gave Karrie a cold stare.

"I don't know." Karrie brushed away the grass Josh had thrown at her. "Maybe living away from your folks isn't as hard as you think. A really wise person once told me things don't always happen like we expect them to, and sometimes that's okay." Lo'laini smiled at Karrie.

"Okay, dude," Josh poked Tom while looking at Lo'laini, "now they're talking in code. So I think we should move on to another subject."

"No code talking is going on. It's just that lots of people live away from their parents, and sometimes it's no big deal," Lo'laini explained.

There was an awkward moment of silence, and then Josh said, "Don't mind Tom. He's a mama's boy. I caught him at youth camp sucking on his thumb and crying on his bed saying he missed his mommy."

"No, dude." Tom smirked. "I think that was you."

"Okay, it could have been me." Josh laughed "My mom makes incredible burritos. I could have been going through a chili withdrawal."

"The only reason Josh is making such slanderous remarks about me is because, well, I'm not sure I should tell you this, but Josh ruined my relationship with my dad," Tom said putting his hand melodramatically across his head.

"Poor baby," said Lo'laini, "how'd he do that?"

"He invited me to church camp, and when I came home and told my dad I wanted to be a Christian, my dad practically disowned me!" explained Tom.

"He did not disown you, Tom. He just told you he was an atheist," said Josh.

"That's right, my dad's an atheist. I can hear you two girls gasp in your hearts."

Karrie laughed, but Lo'laini just rolled her eyes. "I've heard a lot of things about people that are much worse than someone's dad being an atheist," said Lo'laini.

"But not to worry, my dad's not one of those angry atheists. He's one of the intellectual ones. So he's tolerant of my faith. He sat me down after camp and said he was glad that I found something at the church, but he didn't want me to preach about it around the house. So we made a deal."

"Sounds petty healthy to me," said Lo'laini.

"Although . . . " Tom smiled as he sat up. "My grandma says my dad used to claim to be a Christian when he was in high school."

"So what do you think happened?" asked Karrie.

"I don't know. He won't talk about it, but it proves the statement of the day, that things aren't always what they seem."

"The statement Karrie said was that things don't always happen like we expect them to," Lo'laini said, laughing. "If you're going to pronounce it as the statement of the day, then get it right!"

"Well, the principle still applies," said Tom. "Now, my man Josh—he has perfect parents."

"My parents aren't perfect," said Josh.

"His dad is a church deacon and an engineer, and his mom is a school-teacher," Tom loudly whispered, pointing his thumb toward Josh. "You know how this guy became a Christian? His dad prayed with him in the car after church one day!"

"Aww," said Lo'laini and Karrie in unison. "That's so sweet!" added Karrie.

"Sounds pretty perfect to me," said Lo'laini.

"C'mon, Lo'laini, you said your parents are Christians, too," said Josh.

"Yeah, they are. Mom prayed with me, too, when I accepted Christ. It was when my mom had cancer. We went to church one night, and all her friends went and prayed with her at the altar. I saw her face glowing and how her prayer reflected God's love, and I wanted the same love she had for God," Lo'laini said softly.

"That sounds pretty perfect," said Josh.

"Except . . . " Lo'laini paused. "My mom died of cancer, and my dad, well, sometimes my dad struggles with his faith, and that is all I'm going to say about it."

"So is your mom a Christian, Karrie?" asked Tom.

"Yeah, but she still has her struggles. I accepted Christ when Miss Dawn, my Sunday school teacher, prayed with me after she told the story of the prodigal son. When I told my mom after church, she just told me it was fine, and she was glad I did it. But not to get too carried away with it."

"What do you think she meant by that?" asked Josh.

"I don't know, but like I said, I think she struggles with it, too," said Karrie.

"We've all got struggles!" said Tom.

"Some people have bigger struggles than others," Lo'laini added.

Suddenly Josh stood up and nodded at Tom. "You know, I think we should take care of this."

Lo'laini, Tom, and Karrie looked up to see a balding elderly man staggering their way. His clothes were wrinkled, and his face was dirty, as if he had slept on the street the night before. He was clearly drunk, and Lo'laini's face flushed red as the two boys walked up toward him.

"He looks just like Dad used to when he was drunk," Lo'laini whispered to Karrie.

"Lo'laini, that's my old neighbor," whispered Karrie before she ran after Tom and Josh. "No, wait! I know him! He used to be my neighbor."

"Karrie," said Tom, "I don't think you should talk to him—"

"Mr. Pigion," Karrie asked, "are you all right?"

"Do I know you?" slurred the older man.

Karrie nodded.

"I got lost. I get so confused nowadays. Can you please tell me where the bus stop is, young lady?"

"You're walking the wrong way. The bus station is on Park Avenue, and it's behind you down the hill," Karrie calmly said to the man.

"Thank you so much," the old man stammered. He turned around and stumbled down the hill. The three turned around and walked quietly back to the flower shawl on the lawn. No one talked until Karrie did.

"He used to take the number 2 bus and transfer to the 115 to take his wife to Mercy Hospital," said Karrie. "The bus is a funny thing. You really don't know the people around you, but you see them every day making trips to work, school, or to therapy at a hospital. So even though you don't know them, you know about them. His wife had dementia, so she would babble all the way on the bus until it stopped in front of Mercy Hospital. He would gently lead her to her seat in spite of her stubbornness and constant babble, and he would blush red as people would stare at her. Yet he never lost his temper. Sometimes she would slap him, other times she would swear at him, but he was always so kind to her.

"One night, when he got off the bus, the bus driver said, 'Sir, I just want to say to you that I admire you. I admire you so much.' Other people on the bus started to applaud. He smiled shyly and then walked off the bus. I was usually scared to ride the bus at night, but I felt so good and safe on that bus ride home that night. I mean, every night we rode that bus together, acting like we didn't know one another, but in that one moment, when everyone applauded, we all admitted we did know each other. In fact, we cared about each other."

"So what happened to him?" asked Lo'laini. "What happened to her?"

"She died, I guess," said Karrie, shrugging her shoulder. "It's funny. I think we all expected, at least *I* expected, that after his wife died, his life would be so much better. I mean, I thought it was good that he was keeping her together, but we all thought it was such a shame because she was holding him back. He didn't start to smell like brandy until he started to take that bus by himself, alone. That's when I realized it wasn't him who was keeping her together—she was somehow holding him together."

"So," said Tom as he slipped his hand into Karrie's hand, "sometimes things aren't always what they seem be."

"Yeah, and sometimes things don't always happen like we want them to," Karrie said while squeezing Tom's hand.

Chapter 20

"So you girls are going to be on the floor today," Isabella said to Lo'laini and Karrie the next day as they walked into the breakroom before their noon shift began.

"We're hosting a pastor's conference today. It lasts until four p.m. Angela and Natasha are attending a friend's wedding, and they asked if they could leave early, so I thought you two would like to take their place."

"Cool," said Lo'laini as she high-fived Karrie.

"You girls will hit the floor about one forty-five. Lunch and dessert will have already been served by that time. You'll be basically serving coffee during the speaking portion of the event. There will be a full large pot of coffee and one large pot of hot water in the back of the room, in case anyone wants to serve themselves. This afternoon, your job is to walk up and down the aisles between the tables, carrying a carafe of coffee—unobtrusively, mind you—and offer refills of coffee and tea to those listening to the speaker. Wait for them to get your attention. They usually make a slight hand signal. Serve them on their right side, like you were trained. Okay?

"You'll be making those rounds about every five minutes. For the rest of the time, you'll be standing in the back and making sure the coffee is not burning and that there is fresh coffee when needed. The speaker will start about two o'clock. The guests will have a scheduled break at two thirty. So about two twenty-five, you'll have to get fresh-baked goods on the carts from the kitchen and restock the back tables. Most of all, make sure there is fresh coffee at their break time. I don't want anyone saying they had cold and bitter coffee at my restaurant due to overheating. We have a light crowd out front, so until two, I can use you in the stockroom. I need the new lunch specials sheet inserted into each of the menus. The menus are on the back table. Lo'laini, because I've already taught you to how tie sheets on with the ribbon, can you train Karrie?"

"Of course," said Lo'laini.

When Isabella turned her back and left the room, Lo'laini squeezed both of Karrie's arms. "We're in! We're in! We're in!" she squealed, jumping up and down.

"What are we in?" Karrie laughed, pulling away from Lo'laini.

"We're on our way to climbing up to being trained as waitresses! And you know what that means, Karrie? Permanent employment and tips! Lots of little coins that make up dollars above minimum wage. C'mon!"

Lo'laini sat down at the table in the back of the room. "I'll show you how to do this."

"So why do you need extra money?" asked Karrie as she followed Lo'laini to the table. "Your dad seems to buy you everything you need."

"I need the money," Lo'laini said as she pulled a pile of menus in front of her, "because Josh doesn't know it yet, but he is going to ask me to the prom, and I'm going to look good when he picks me up."

"So your dad would pay, wouldn't he?"

"I'm showing my dad how independent, I am. How little trouble I am to have around, you know," Lo'laini said as she sat down and reached into the drawer beneath the table and grabbed a handful of red, white, and green ribbons.

"I think Isabella thinks you're better at this job than I am," said Karrie. "She always seems to train you before me."

"She trains me because I ask." Lo'laini laughed as she picked up half the menus in her pile and placed them before Karrie. "Girl, you don't get anything in this world if you don't ask. My dad dropped me off early yesterday. I was sitting in the breakroom waiting for my shift to start, and

Isabella was cutting up ribbons for the menus. I asked her if she wanted us to help put the menus together. I didn't think she'd say yes, but she said if I had a few minutes, she'd show me how it's done. Karrie, I see kids, and even adults, come into this place all the time asking for jobs. We have to show Alejandro and Isabella we're indispensable. We're already trained, so they don't have to bother with us, and we know the place and how it works. This job might not pay millions, but it pays something! And I want to keep working through the school year for extra cash. And you know what they say, 'you can't close a door on someone if they've put their foot in that door.'"

"So you just ask, huh? You mean, you asked Alejandro and Isabella—you don't ask any of the guys in back kitchen, do ya?"

"Miguel and his crew! Ugh!" Lo'laini shook her body as if she was shaking something off. "I make it my policy never to speak to anyone who might be currently residing under a rock. Besides, they're not going to let us do anything in the kitchen anyway. All those guys are trained chefs. The only reason we got to prepare our dessert was because it was good publicity for the restaurant to do something with the high school. But if I could get a good reference out of this place, that might pry that door open in the future—if we make a good impression."

Lo'laini grabbed a menu and started to string the ribbon in the back holes on the top. "This is simple. It has to be done once a week, so if we do it well, we might have a few extra hours on our paycheck. Watch me. You simply string the ribbon through the back side and tie a bow attaching this week's lunch specials on the menu. When you tie the bow, make sure the loops point upward and the tails point downward. Just like"—Lo'laini's fingers skillfully made the bow—"that!"

It took Karrie and Lo'laini forty-five minutes to compile the menus. Then Isabella came in to tell them they were wanted on the main floor so they headed to the guest room. Angela and Natasha were waiting for them right inside the door of the guest room. Their faces brightened as they saw the girls approaching.

"Thanks, you guys, for doing this," whispered Angela, loosening her apron as she was walking out of the room.

"Yeah," said Natasha. "It's going to take a while for me to make that teal dress look good." She smiled.

"It's not a bad dress," said Angela. "I mean, if you were going to the prom in 1996. But it's her wedding. She gets to choose the dress. It's just the third formal teal dress I've bought that I won't ever be able to wear again—but at least the reception will be fun! Anyway, both of you have nothing to worry about. These guys are pretty easy. They have this conference once a year, and they are really polite and not too demanding. I know Isabella told you to walk in between the aisles, but I wouldn't do that. There is some kind of argument going on between the group. So instead stand in the back and let yourself be seen, and they'll signal you if they want a refill. I wouldn't get between them just now."

"Amen!" Natasha laughed as she pulled her friend away and out the back door. "Never let yourself get in a fight between customers. See ya later!"

As soon as Lo'laini and Karrie took their places on either side of the long table that held two large silver coffeepots, a man turned around and raised his porcelain cup slightly toward Lo'laini.

Lo'laini picked up the small carafe and walked confidently toward the man to fill his cup. Afterward, she held up her pot graciously, smiling at people sitting in the general vicinity, and some beckoned her to come over to top off their cups.

Karrie's stomach hurt while she was looking at Lo'laini. Adults frightened Karrie most of the time, and yet her friend always acted so professional and confident around them. It seemed like a simple task—to carry a coffeepot across the room and pour a cup of coffee; but Karrie wasn't sure she would be able to pull this thing off. What if she tripped or spilled the coffee, or even worse, dropped the pot? What if someone got angry and yelled at her?

Soon a woman sitting at a table near the back caught Karrie's eye and raised her cup. Karrie walked over and filled her cup. Then she walked to the back of the room and stood at her station. She sighed with relief. *Okay, that wasn't hard. No spills.* Another man beside the woman raised his cup, and Karrie quickly filled it. Then she walked back to her station, and Lo'laini smiled at her. *Easy as pie,* she mouthed to Karrie.

Another man near the front turned around and smiled at Karrie, holding up his cup. This man was talking to the speaker as Karrie began to fill his cup.

"What troubles me about this conversation," said the elderly man as he put down his cup and smiled graciously at Karrie, "is that we are talking about a serious breach in confidence of the pastoral office."

A woman beside the man motioned to Karrie. "Miss, please," she whispered while holding up her cup.

"You mean having a window in your office is a breach of your confidence?" asked the woman standing in front of the room. "Is there a need for such a confidence between a pastor and parishioner?"

With a single groan, the room affirmed there was indeed such a need.

Karrie walked back to her station.

"What I meant to say was, should anyone be visiting the pastor secretly?" The speaker paused and then continued, "You know that could be perceived by some parishioners as suspicious."

"Dr. Kisbey, why should all congregants suffer because there are some pastors who don't behave appropriately? There are times I need to talk alone with a congregant and there are times someone wants to talk alone to a minister. I think we are talking too much about professional people protecting themselves and not enough about professionals taking personal responsibility.

"Opportunity does not equal violation. By the time a pastor abuses their congregant, they've gone through a lot of mental rationalizations to legitimize their behavior. In other words, they have believed a lot of lies that have told them they have the right to abuse someone. I think certain attitudes toward women provide fertile ground for harassment, and I think we need to be examining those attitudes if we want to talk about abuse."

The woman behind the man motioned for Karrie to fill her cup, and while Karrie was filling her cup, the woman said to the speaker, "I think your examples are all from the man's perspective." Her face was flushed red, and her voice was trembling as she spoke. "Each of the examples you have given today have presented women as the aggressor, and I find your attempt at humor insulting."

"And frankly," continued the elder man in front of her, "I found the skit you did of a pastor visiting a widow offensive. I wonder if you have ever been in the presence of a grieving widow. Yes, a minister should exercise wisdom in his pastoral visits by taking an elder or deacon along on a visit, but I think any pastor who blames pastoral visits as an excuse for their sexual scandals is simply shifting blame. If clergy cannot trust themselves in a room alone with a parishioner, perhaps they should consider if they have any business in the ministry to begin with. It would trouble me deeply if any pastors stopped making pastoral visits because of this training or stopped picking up the elderly or children for church. There is always the option of taking a chaperone with you. And I agree, your examples of parishioners coming on to pastors are a little misogynistic. Women are the aggressors in each of your skits. You have yet to present an instant where a pastor misuses authority on parishioners."

"But I understand what the doctor is saying," said a younger man in front, motioning to Lo'laini to fill his cup. "She is simply saying we ought not to be putting ourselves at risk by being alone with vulnerable people, and I think it may be wise advice. You know, Jesus spent most of His time among the crowds, not with individuals."

"You're forgetting the woman at the well," said the older man. "I would remind my fellow clergy that Jesus set the precedence of treating women as equals by speaking to them publicly and meeting with them privately. Jesus also met alone with Nicodemus, because Nicodemus was frightened of the religious leaders. People have similar fears today."

Another man on Karrie's side signaled her, and she started to walk past a man who impatiently turned on the man who was just speaking.

A young man spoke with an agitated voice. "We're supposed to be talking about sexual scandal, and let's be honest here by saying it is not always wise to spend time alone with emotionally needy women."

The man behind Karrie said, "I am sorry, call me politically incorrect, but with the way ministry is today, I don't think any male pastor should ever be alone with any woman. You're being naïve if you do so."

Karrie walked quickly back to her station.

"Son, we're living in 2019," the elderly man replied. "It doesn't matter who you are alone with, some people are going to complain. I've been in the ministry for thirty-five years and knew about pastors who behaved inappropriately and were quietly sent away to counseling instead of anyone talking about the patterns in their lives. This isn't new. We're just talking openly about it now! There have always been pastors who don't behave like pastors when they should, and there has always been self-sacrificing pastors who have behaved well, treating men and women as equal children of God. Again, I think someone who misbehaves will do so whether there is a window or not. I think we should be looking at attitudes towards women not about the arrangement of office decor. And personally, I think we've made too many excuses for ministers that have behaved badly. We send them away to Christian counseling and then send them back into ministry. Sometimes jail was needed not a trip to a counselor."

"But we're not talking about sexual scandal," said another woman from across the room. "We're talking about harassment. Sexual scandal and harassment are not the same things. Harassment involves the misuse of power, a subject we have not adequately addressed."

The woman sitting directly in front of the man held up her cup while looking at Karrie and said, "I guess that is what bothers me the most from this conversation. When I worked in a lawyer's office before, I went to a seminary. Whenever we talk about sexual harassment, we talk about power and control. The lawyers were asked to consider their attitudes about women and their misuse of their power." She put down her cup and looked directly at the speaker. "I guess that's why I am so disappointed in this training. Once again, the secular world is doing so much better than we are in their thinking on this subject. Not once have we talked about a pastor misusing power. Instead, we are talking about 'emotionally needy women' and ways male pastors can protect themselves from those women and not the other way around?

"Let me make myself clear, Dr. Kisbey. The examples you are giving today are ostracizing women from pastoral counseling and leadership in the church by blaming women for what men do. But that is hardly a new thought, I'm sorry to say."

There was a small applause from the women in the crowd.

"Okay," said a younger man up front, "aren't you the ones who are being bigoted? It's not always men who abuse women. There has been some recent news I could bring up of a couple cases of women teachers who have behaved inappropriately."

"Okay, point taken. There are some cases of women who are perpetrators," said a woman, who was clearly emotionally moved by the conversation. She beckoned Karrie to come and fill her cup while she continued to speak. "But it doesn't happen as often to men as it does to women; it is rare. Dr. Kisbey, women are two to one to experience sexual harassment in society. We haven't addressed the way men think about women and how they view their power when they begin to harass someone who is working for them."

"So if I understand you correctly, you seem to think I am blaming the victim. No, I don't mean to blame the victim, if that *is* what you're implying. I did want to make the point that it happens to males as well as to women, and

I am urging that the pastor should be cautious," Dr. Kisbey replied. "I do think victims of harassment should be treated with compassion."

"I prefer the term *survivor*," said the woman sitting in front. "Actually, the Department of Justice reports that seventeen percent of women claim they have been harassed in their lifetime as opposed to just three percent of men. I've worked in this field for many years and as a pastoral counselor, and I am troubled about how this training is playing out this afternoon. As Christian ministers, I agree we should be talking more about the attitudes that cause sexual harassment and less about protecting our backsides."

Karrie saw another man in the back who motioned for her. As she walked past the agitated man, he angrily replied to the woman, "Sin causes the behavior, and that will always exist! But I want to be clear about what I mean about sin—it is sin in both parties. Where are all these victims of abuse the statistics talk about? I've never met one of them. Thank you, miss," he said to Karrie as she finished filling his cup.

Then he continued, "I am sick of all this talk that always makes one person the predator and the other the victim! Some women give signals, and they can't blame someone when they respond to their signals."

"I certainly would hold a pastor accountable!" said the older man angrily.

"Come on, Larry! What would you tell a teenager who told you he got signals? You would tell the young man that regardless of the signals, he was still responsible for his behavior. So many people are wounded by violation in the church that I find it trivializing to talk about signals."

Karrie quickly returned to her station; she was shaking now. Lo'laini walked over and stood by her.

"They're not talking about you, Karrie," whispered Lo'laini. "You're always telling me to calm down. Now it's my turn to tell you, don't let this get you upset."

Someone motioned to Lo'laini, and she walked across the room to fill a cup. "If sin is the problem," continued the elder man, "then we have the solution. The solution is confession, contrition, repentance, and accountability. I agree with my Christian sister on the other side of the room. We need to have an honest discussion about how women have been wrongly perceived in the church. In my ministry, I've grown weary of the number of women I have seen beaten up and misused in the name of submission. I don't think that was the example Christ left us in how to treat women. I believe that was a reason that Jesus spent so much time with women who were oppressed on this earth. It was because He knew about their pain."

"You know, I get tired of all the victim talk," said the younger man. "I don't see women as downtrodden as popular culture makes them out to be. Statistics can be manipulated, and a lot of people cry rape and harassment to get attention. For example, I think it is too easy for kids to report their parents. It's tearing families apart in this country, and I stand for family values. I know some of you are going be angry at me for saying this, but it is the easiest thing in the world for a woman to cry rape. As far as the supposed pain of 'abuse and harassment,' I think people who have been abused need to take responsibility for their pain. I believe the greatest lesson someone who has been abused can learn is to forgive. If they would simply forgive and move on, they wouldn't find themselves in so much pain. What we need is restoration of the traditional family, and that would solve most of the abuse problems in this world. "

"Harassment and abuse are not family values," said the woman who had been seated in the front of the room as she got up from chair and walked angrily toward the back of the room. She folded her arms across her chest and leaned against the wall.

"Of course, that's not what I meant," said the younger man.

"But that's how a lot of people take it," said another man close to the door. "I've heard men use the teaching of submission to beat women up emotionally in public and, I suspect, physically, in private. There is an issue here, brothers and sisters, about how wrongly interpreted the teaching of submission has kept women in subservient roles that make them more susceptible to abuse."

"I think we've gotten off the topic!" said Dr. Kisbey. "But I must admit, perhaps my examples have been wrongly interpreted. So allow me to make myself clear. I don't believe people should be blamed when they have been victimized because someone else has misused their office."

"We're not off topic," said the older woman in the back of the room. "Harassment and abuse are crimes of power against the powerless."

"Well, with the way young women dress today," said a timid older woman in the front row, "I don't think there is enough talk about women taking responsibility for the way they dress and how some come on to a man. Even when we talk about children, we don't talk enough about their responsibility in the abuse. In fact, I think, how old the child is could be an indicator as to whether abuse really occurred or if there was any mutual consent!"

Some people in the room grumbled against that last remark, but Karrie could not hear them. She had been trembling throughout the conversation. She had leaned against the wall to steady herself. That last remark hit Karrie like a punch to the stomach and knocked the air out of her. She felt her fingers loosen on the carafe she was holding, and it fell to the floor. It bounced once before lying on its side in the center of the room. The spilled coffee immediately stained the carpet in a half circle across the room. Everyone in the room seemed to stand up in unison and turn around to look at the trembling young server who now had two tear stained black streaks of mascara running down her cheeks to her chin.

"Miss," said the elderly man who had been sitting in front of the conference room, "are you okay?"

Karrie couldn't answer. She just stood there looking at them, and they stood quietly looking at her. Time stood still in an awkward suffocating silence. Then Isabella's voice calmed the room.

"Everything is under control," she said as she placed her hand on Karrie's shoulder. "Please excuse us and continue your conference."

Then she turned to the young man behind her. "Antonio, why don't you clean up this mess, and you can take Karrie's spot in the dining room while she helps me in the stockroom," whispered Isabella. "Come along, Karrie."

Karrie was quiet until they reached the stockroom, and then she broke down into tears.

"Please don't fire me!" she cried out between sobs. "I am so sorry! Please don't fire me! I need this job. I want this job. Please don't fire me!"

"No one is going to fire you, Karrie," whispered Isabella in a motherly tone as she handed Karrie a towel. "Dry your tears." She placed a box of saltshakers on the table

"Now we need to fill the saltshakers for tomorrow's guests. You simply twist off the top of the shakers and hold the shaker between your finger and thumb near the rim, like I am doing. Fill them up until salt reaches the place where your thumb is grasping the container. Do you understand?"

Karrie nodded and began to twist off the tops of the shakers.

"You know, Karrie," said Isabella as her fingers nimbly unscrewed the saltshaker tops, "people say a lot of stupid things when they come to a Mexican restaurant. I know it is hard to believe someone may be so uncouth as to make racist statements about someone who is serving them dinner. Or that they would make crude remarks about people who labor ten to fifteen hours in the fields in conditions that the customer would not survive ten minutes working under . . . and all that work so they have fresh fruit and vegetables on their table. But customers make those remarks. For some, they think it is part of their dining-out experience in an ethnic restaurant to make racist jokes. Some people feel that because they are in a Mexican restaurant, they are entitled to purposely speak bad Spanish and make cruel remarks about a fine culture. You know, I had one man ask me if I had a green card?"

Isabella looked up at Karrie.

"That man didn't know I had a business degree from Brown University and that I was buying this restaurant instead of just working as a server. It wouldn't have mattered if he did know it, because he thought he was making a joke and I was the one who should be a good sport about his demeaning remark. He knew my tip was dependent upon it."

Isabella took the shakers Karrie had finished filling and put them in a red box beside her. She set another handful of shakers in front of Karrie.

"So do you know what I do when someone says something stupid or cruel about ethnicity when I am serving them?" she asked.

Karrie wasn't sure if she should answer, so she simply kept quiet.

"I ask them if they would like anything from the bar to complement their meal, or I ask them if they would like to try our Tres Leche cake. Then at the end of the evening, I ask them how they would like to pay, and then . . . " Isabella paused and smiled and said, "I take their money."

"But don't those words hurt you?" Karrie asked.

"Oh yes." Isabella looked directly into Karrie's eyes. "They break my heart and they wound my spirit. But I let them pass. Do you know why I do that, Karrie? Because I am at work, and there is a time and a place for certain dialogue, and I am not going to allow their ignorance and bigotry to destroy my passions and my work."

Isabella stood up and brushed the extra salt off her uniform.

"Now, Karrie, put your finished saltshakers into the red box and pick up some menus and follow me."

Karrie followed Isabella out to the reception area where she handed her menus to Isabella, who placed them into a wooden slot by the reception podium.

The twenty-three-year-old receptionist smiled when she saw Isabella enter the room. Karrie noticed that underneath her waitress uniform was a teal puffy slip. She had clearly anxiously been watching the clock and tapping her fingers on the podium before Karrie and Isabella entered the room.

"Carmen, you look distracted," Isabella said.

"Well, the wedding, you know. I was hoping I could get off early today."

Isabella smiled at the receptionist

"Okay, Carmen, why don't you take the rest of the day off? I know you were invited to the wedding as well, and if you hurry, you can make it to the reception." Isabella waved her off.

"Oh, Isabella, you're a saint! A saint!" Carmen hugged Isabella.

"Not a saint, just practical," Isabella shrugged her shoulders as Carmen turned around to walk out the back door, Isabella handed Karrie a pair of rubber gloves and a small trash bag.

"We try to check this area every half hour for trash and paper people toss on the floor. Do you see those two potted plants in the back? One is a cactus, and the other is called a desert rose. Some people think it is witty to hide their trash in the pots. So we need to clean them out at least twice a day."

Karrie put on the gloves and began to scoop out wads of chewing gum, small candy wrappers, and cigarette butts while Isabella swept the floor. When Karrie finished, she handed the trash bag she had filled to Isabella. As she did so, she noticed a picture over Isabella's shoulder of a dignified woman smiling compassionately. The woman's broad frame and warm smile captivated Karrie, and she couldn't take her eyes off the picture.

Isabella took the bag from Karrie. "Do you know who these people are?" She pointed to the wall behind Karrie's back.

"No, I'm sorry, I never noticed them before. In the past, I only noticed—" Karrie started to say, but Isabella interrupted her.

"You only noticed sombreros, maracas, guitarron, and the lace mantilla. We also have pictures between them. People see what they want to see. I wish people would notice these pictures more. The woman who is on the far corner is Maria Moreno, she worked for fair pay for agricultural workers and later became a Pentecostal minister. The woman above is Rigoberta Menchu, and she is from Quiché, Guatemala. She is an activist for peace, and she was awarded the Nobel Peace Prize in 1992 for her work in peacemaking in South America. The man whose picture is in the upper right corner—his name is Luis Palau. He is an evangelist in South America. Some people say he preached to greater crowds than Billy Graham. The center picture is of Gabriel García Márquez. He is the 1982 Nobel Prize winner for literature, and his works have been translated into dozens of languages. The man in the picture in the left corner is Edwin Bustillos. He was an agricultural engineer from the Sierra Madre in Mexico. He has worked tirelessly to conserve desert plant life and to destroy the drug cartel in Mexico."

Karrie stood with her eyes fixed on the pictures of heroes on the restaurant wall.

"Karrie, do you know why your dessert was served at this restaurant?" Isabella quietly asked. "I am sorry to say it wasn't your cooking ability." Isabella then laughed and put her arm around Karrie. "It was the proposal you wrote. You have a way with words. Your descriptions caught both Alejandro's and my eyes. You have a way with words, Karrie."

Isabella looked back at the restaurant wall. "Do you know what all these people have in common, Karrie, besides passion and talent? They've all been criticized and misunderstood. I believe God gives passion and talent. The world gives us unfair criticism. But God wins when we allow His passion and talent to override the world's criticism. I have a wall, Karrie, to express my passion, and I have a kitchen to express my talent. Karrie, you have a voice, and you've got to start using it."

"I can't spell," said Karrie, still mesmerized by the pictures she had never seen before this minute.

"People have overcome greater obstacles," said Isabella as she straightened a picture of Cesar Chavez. "Karrie, it doesn't take a psychology degree to see someone has hurt you very badly and there are tears inside of you screaming out to the world to be heard. Lots of people have those tears. If you want to survive in this world, you are going to have to find a way to make sure those tears don't rule your life. You find the words that represent your tears, and then you share those words to the world. I have my wall; you find your words."

"I didn't know you were training in the reception area tonight?"

Isabella and Karrie turned around to see Alejandro behind them.

"I'm always training," said Isabella. "I think it is my favorite part of my job."

Chapter 21

The following Wednesday night after youth group, Karrie stood trembling in front of the microphone in the sanctuary.

"Okay." Pastor Mike waved his arms at Karrie, who was standing in the middle aisle. "Don't be frightened. Just keep your head up and look at the back wall and speak directly into the microphone."

"Hello," Karrie said as the microphone let out a squeal.

"Tom, get away from the soundboard." Pastor Mike wrinkled his brow and looked squarely at Tom who immediately took his hands off the controls on the soundboard.

"I was just trying to help," he said, blushing.

"Well, you were not helping, Tom," said Pastor Mike, shaking his head. Turning to Karrie he said, "Just remember, everyone that will be here in church Sunday morning wants you to succeed. You don't have any enemies in our congregation. If it helps you, find a familiar face and look at them while you're sharing your testimony."

"Yeah!" Lo'laini waved from the third pew where she was sitting with Josh. "We'll be sitting right here, so just look at us and we'll keep you focused."

"Whatever you do . . . " Pastor Mike laughed. "Don't look at the people in the third pew. They'll just make you laugh."

"Hey," said Tom, "I resent that remark."

"Not a new joke." Lo'laini rolled her eyes.

"Why don't you try to read a Bible verse and see how your voice sounds with the mic," Pastor Mike suggested. "Have you chosen the Scripture you're going to share?"

"No," Karrie fumbled through the Bible in front of her. "I haven't figured that out yet."

"I've got one," Lo'laini held up her smart phone. "I put the word *testimony* into the search box on the online Bible, and this verse came up— Revelations 12:11."

"Why don't you look that verse up and read it out loud, Karrie," said Pastor Mike.

Karrie fumbled through the Bible on the podium and found the verse. "'And they overcame the evil one because of the blood of the Lamb, and because of the word of their testimony,'" Karrie read aloud. "Hey, the microphone didn't squeak that time."

"Bravo! Bravo!" Lo'laini, Tom, and Josh broke out in applause.

Karrie did a small curtsy. "'The power of their testimony,'" she read the phrase again. "So what does that mean, Pastor Mike?"

"It's the power of our experience in the spoken word," Pastor Mike said thoughtfully. "I was thinking about this verse today during an outreach meeting at church we were having about publicity. I really like this Scripture."

"Hey, you're a preacher." Tom laughed. "You're supposed to like *all* the Scriptures."

"I do." Pastor Mike leaned against the pew and opened pulled out a Bible next to him and turned to the text. "'But some minister to me more than others.' This is a verse about the last days. The people in this Scripture died for their faith, and when they reached heaven, a voice proclaimed they had overcome the evil one by their witness. Their witness was their testimony. So what was their witness? God had not rescued them from death, yet they still had a witness about the faithfulness of God. You have to think about that part of it."

"Like the Christians refugees fleeing Syria and Egypt," Tom said quietly.

"Yeah," whispered Karrie coming down from the podium. "I think a lot about the kids in those countries when I think about what happened to me."

A hush of reverence seemed to fall over the four highschoolers as Pastor Mike went on to explain.

"Those things are hard to think about. Those things are ugly to look at. When I think about situations like yours, I know we need to depend on God's grace to offer comfort where we cannot. The victors—the Scriptures call them the overcomers in the book of Revelations—they were not pretty and successful people. The people who had the greatest testimony were the people whom God did not rescue, but gave them the strength to endure their death."

"So, why were you thinking about it in the outreach meeting?" asked Lo'laini.

"The committee decided to hire a bunch of models for the billboard we're placing on the freeway. They will be using the models rather than our real church members." Pastor Mike wearily closed his Bible.

"That's messed up." Tom poised showing flexing his muscles. "You mean we aren't pretty enough?"

"Apparently not," said Pastor Mike, shaking his head.

"Maybe they were just trying to make it slick and professional." Lo'laini smiled.

"That's exactly what they were trying to do." Pastor Mike sighed. "But the reality is that Christianity isn't always slick and professional. God's grace can be messy and mysterious . . ."

"Full of unanswered questions," Karrie completed Pastor Mike's sentence, and he smiled warmly at her.

"Personally, the moments I experienced God's grace the greatest have been moments when I've been the least slick and professional." Pastor Mike motioned over to the sanctuary side window to the people leaving the evening

Bible study. "Most of the people in this church have the same testimony. They came here because they were accepted. Slick and professional images are not the best way for a church to grow."

"So did you tell them that?" Tom asked.

"Nope." Pastor Mike put his hands in his pockets and raised his eyebrows. "I guess I didn't have the words at that moment to say what I really believed."

"What did you want to say?" Tom asked.

"No, that's not the way you ask that question," Lo'laini interrupted. She got up from her seat in the pew, and she twisted her hair into a tightly knotted bun and stuck a pencil through the center.

"So there's a wrong way to ask a question?" Tom asked.

"Yeah, there is." Lo'laini laughed as she put on a pair of reading glasses. "It's therapy time, and I can show you how the professionals do it. I've been through it enough in foster care." She turned her head to the side and in a contrived compassionate voice asked, "How did that make you feel?"

"It makes me feel you should lose the hairdo and the glasses." Pastor Mike wrinkled his forehead, showing his annoyance. "Where did you get those glasses?"

"They were on the pew." Lo'laini laughed again.

"Please hand them over." Pastor Mike reached out his hand to take the glasses. "I think they belong to Mrs. Abiola."

"She's the lady that works in the school cafeteria," said Josh.

"She's also the lady that fled from Christian persecution and poverty in Congo to give her children a better life here in America." Pastor Mike looked tenderly at the battered pair of faded black plastic-framed glasses. "What I wish I said—what I should've said—was that the people who fled to Jesus in the first century wouldn't have fit well in any modeling shot. Those early Christians would face three hundred years of persecution after Jesus left. In Scripture and in life, God's glory shines in the testimony of people whom God had preserved through trials. The fact that God didn't rescue them isn't a great selling point from our perspective. Their suffering wouldn't sell very well on a billboard. It isn't pretty, but Christianity isn't always pretty. Sometimes it is the unanswered prayers and unanswered questions that bring God the greatest glory. At least, in my ministry, I have found when people voice their doubts, it unleashes God's greatest healing."

"But don't you think people want to hear happy stories instead of sad ones when you're trying to win someone over to Christ?" asked Lo'laini.

"I'm sorry to say, it's not where most people live, Lo'laini," said Pastor Mike. "Don't get me wrong, life has great moments of great happiness and joy, and I suppose there are some people who are tremendously successful and never had a moment of doubt or fear that plagued them. But most people are haunted by moments of tragedy, either in their life or from something in history. So God gave us a Savior who walks people through those times, who touches ordinary people who are scared by sin and disappointment. These are ordinary people, not airbrushed models that look like they never had a pimple or a flaw in their life."

"Dude, it's not Sunday. Stop preaching." Tom laughed.

Pastor Mike wrapped his arm around Tom's head in a half nelson and used his knuckles to mess up his hair. "As long as I'm your pastor, I'll preach to you as much as I want."

Tom squirmed to get out of Pastor Mike's hold while Pastor Mike and everyone else laughed, except for Karrie. Pastor Mike's words resounded inside of her. They struck her in the center of her heart, but she could not say why.

Pastor Mike loosened his hold on Tom, who shook himself loose. "This is all too profound for me, and I want some tacos."

"All right, you guys, I've got to lock up tonight," said Pastor Mike.

"Some of the kids are meeting at the taco shop down the street, if you want to join them."

"Hey." Tom looked around in astonishment. "It's a miracle! None of us are working tonight! So let's go persecute some of the kids that are!"

"Now *that* is not the spirit I wanted to nurture," Pastor Mike said, waving the group out.

"We'll get the car, girls, if you want to meet us out front." Josh pulled out his keys.

As Karrie descended from the podium, she shoved a small piece of paper into her pocket.

"Another poem?" asked Lo'laini as she walked up to Karrie.

"Don't tease me. Josh writes you poems, too," retorted Karrie.

"He does not!" Lo'laini tried to grab the paper from Karrie's hands.

"Yeah, he did," laughed Karrie as both the girls walked down the middle aisle toward the door. "When he left those plumeria flowers by your locker, I remember he left a poem on a piece of paper."

They were now outside in front of the church. "You mean he wrote me one poem," said Lo'laini as she sat down on the church's front stairs. "Do you know what that poem said? 'Roses are red, violets are blue, I want to be romantic, and so this poem I do.'"

"Well, it has imagery and it rhymes, so you could say it was a poem," laughed Karrie looking around for the boys.

"You could say it was a *wannabe* poem." Lo'laini rolled her eyes.

"At least he got the plumeria flowers right."

"Yes, plumerias," Lo'laini said thoughtfully. "Grandma used to say they were the lace of the islands." *Aoogah! Aoogah!*

"What was that!" both girls said in unison.

As they turned their heads, Josh's 2001 White Ford Festiva rounded the corner and pulled up in front of the girls. The back seat was covered with gardenias and daisies. Both side mirrors had flowered leis hanging over the sides. Tom was hanging out the side window with an air horn in his hand. He squeezed it again.

"Aoogah!" the horn screamed.

Lo'laini let out an involuntary squeal.

"Girl," shouted Karrie, "I have never heard a sound like that come out of your mouth before."

"What can I say?" Lo'laini smiled. "The boy got it right this time."

"You've trained him well, Lo'laini," laughed Karrie. Both girls glowed with approval at the newly-decorated car. Then they both heard the screech of tires on their other side. It was Lo'laini's father's truck. It had pulled up onto the sidewalk.

"Loni! Loni! What's the matter with you, girl? I've been looking all over for you." Lo'laini's father shouted as he stumbled out of the car. He staggered toward both the girls. His shirt was crookedly buttoned and was only half-shoved into his jeans. His whole being smelled of beer and weed.

Lo'laini quickly turned and ran to her father. "Dad, it's okay. I'm here. You don't need to shout. You knew I'd be here for youth group tonight, remember, Dad?" She tried to quiet her father.

"Don't hush me, girl," her father shouted. "Don't you ever hush me. It's not Sunday, why are you at church on Wednesday? You spend too much time here, girl." Lo'laini's father's words slurred together.

"Like I said, it's youth group, Dad," said Lo'laini. "You remember youth group? It takes place on Wednesday night."

"No, I don't remember, Loni," shouted Lo'laini's father. "You hurt me, Lo'laini, you know that? You hurt me."

"How have I hurt you?" said Lo'laini, still trying to quiet her father.

"You locked up your mother's things. You locked them up so I couldn't get them! Don't lie to me, girl. I know you did it!" His eyes teared up. "You're trying to keep her memory away from me! You always came between her and me. I know that is what you are still trying to do." He raised his hand to hit Lo'laini, but she caught his hand in hers before it landed on her.

"Daddy," she whispered, "please don't, Daddy. Not here. Not in front of my friends. It's okay, really, it is. Mom's things are in her old filing cabinet on the back terrace." Lo'laini was trying to gently push her father back toward the truck.

"But it's locked, Lo'laini. I've tried the drawer, and it's locked," he cried.

"It's not locked," pleaded Lo'laini. "You just have to push the button in on the side when you pull open the drawer. I'll come home with you, Dad, and I'll show you. It'll be okay, I promise." Lo'laini started to walk back toward the truck with her father, but Josh stood in their way.

"Excuse me, sir," Josh said, stammering, "I'm wondering if you would let me drive Lo'laini back to her house tonight?"

"Are you embarrassed to ride with me, Loni?" asked Lo'laini's father.

"No," said Lo'laini. "I'll see you Friday, Josh."

Josh grabbed Lo'laini's arm. "Lo'laini, don't get in that car. Not with the way he is." He tried to draw Lo'laini aside, but she pushed him away.

"What do you mean 'the way he is'!" Lo'laini shouted at Josh. "He's my dad, you understand that?"

"Lo'laini, think about what's going on here," pleaded Josh.

"Nothing is going on here," said Lo'laini. "Maybe something is going on with you, huh?" She put both hands on Josh's chest and shoved him with all her might. "You have something to say, you punk? Do you have something to say about my dad? Say it to me. Say it to me now! Don't whisper it behind my back like you're so noble that you can feel sorry for me . . ."

"Lo'laini, you know he can't drive. I just don't want you to get hurt because of his condition . . ."

"What condition?" Lo'laini shoved Josh backward again. "Say it! Say it, punk! I dare you! His condition? I'll tell you my dad's condition." Lo'laini's voice was quivering with emotion. "He's tired after working sometimes ten hours a day, and he's grieving . . . he's grieving for my mom 'cause she's not here anymore, and he still has nightmares because of that stupid war! That's my dad's condition!"

"Don't get so upset. Everyone's looking," pleaded Karrie, who had now joined Josh in blocking Lo'laini's way. "You're drawing a crowd."

"What crowd?" Lo'laini asked incredulously.

She looked around at some of the church members who had come out of their Bible study when they heard the shouting on the church patio. The parental concern on the adults' faces burned through Lo'laini as condemnation. Mrs. Abiola came out of the crowd holding her worn Bible to her chest. Her large dark eyes reflected the compassion that only a thousand violations could inspire. But all Lo'laini felt was judgment, and she screamed back at her.

"Hey, lady, why don't you take a picture? It'll last longer!"

"Lo'laini!" Karrie gasped. She stepped forward so she was directly blocking Lo'laini's path to her dad.

"Don't do this, Karrie." Lo'laini stuck out her lower jaw as she spoke. "Don't come between me and my dad."

As Karrie, Lo'laini, and Josh were talking, Pastor Mike walked up to Lo'laini's father. He introduced himself and shook his hand and started to subtly lead him away from the truck until Lo'laini ran up and got between them.

"It's okay, Pastor Mike. My dad's just picking me up. There were some chores I forgot to do, so I'm going to go home with him now."

"Lo'laini . . . ," Pastor Mike started to say, but she quickly cut him off.

"He's not begging the church for any money or anything, so don't treat him like that. He has a right to be here to pick up his own daughter." Lo'laini grabbed her father's arm. "What is *wrong* with you people?"

"Why's everyone so upset?" Lo'laini's father said in bewilderment.

"It's okay, Dad," Lo'laini put her hand on her father's back while opening the driver's door for her father. "We're going home. You're right. I spend too much time at this church anyway."

Karrie stood frozen with fear, feeling her feet glued to the ground as she watched the white truck swerve out of the church parking lot and into the blasting horns of the busy street. "I feel like we should . . . could've done something to stop them, but I can't figure out what," she said nervously.

"There's something we can do," Pastor Mike pulled out his cell phone. "Yes, I would like to report a drunk driver who just left the church's parking lot with a minor in his car. He's going west to get on the freeway."

After the scene at church, Karrie went home feeling sick, with her face flushed in a mixture of shame and hurt. She didn't know why she was hurt and embarrassed. Pastor Mike tried to talk to her, telling her there was nothing to be embarrassed or ashamed about. He told her many people in the church suffered from addiction, and many more had parents or children who were addicts.

"They came out of their study because they were concerned, not to judge you or Lo'laini," Pastor Mike said.

Karrie listened politely, but she didn't believe a word he said. There was no way those nice church people could know what Lo'laini and she had been through. No one talked on the ride home. Both Josh and Tom seemed upset, but they didn't know what to say to Karrie, so they blasted some hip hop music while each one of them was held captive in their thoughts.

When Karrie got home, Mama was counting out her tips on the living room table. "Had a good time at church, dear?" she asked, not looking up from the coins.

"Yeah, Mom, I did," said Karrie as she walked quietly around her mother. "I'm going to bed. I'm not feeling well. I think I might be coming down with the flu."

"Well, you know it's going around." Karrie's mother started another stack of quarters. "Go to bed and get some rest."

Karrie walked to her room and climbed right into bed. She didn't even change into her pajamas. She buried her head into her pillow. Everything about Lo'laini's father had reminded her about her own father, and it hurt her. It hurt her that Lo'laini may have known the same pain she knew.

She stared at the white bear she had received four years earlier in the police station. It was sitting on top of her dresser with its fat belly and wide arms extended like those of a detached, serene Buddha. The bear sat under her bedroom window, the bright moon shining on the bear's head, with the bear's pink smile hidden in the shadow of its long nose.

"It must be frightening to have the night take your voice away," Karrie whispered to the bear.

Chapter 22

Mama woke her up early in the morning. Pastor Mike had called last night after Karrie had fallen asleep. There had been a car accident, and Lo'laini was in the in the hospital. Mama didn't want to wake her up last night, but she said Karrie could skip school that morning to see Lo'laini. Mama rode the bus with her down to the hospital.

When Karrie saw Pastor Mike in the lobby, Mama asked Karrie if she would like to visit Lo'laini alone with Pastor Mike.

Karrie smiled at Mama; she wasn't usually that in tune to Karrie's feelings. "Yes," Karrie said, and Mama went to the cafeteria to get something to eat while Karrie and Pastor Mike sat in the waiting room. Pastor Mike picked up his Bible that was on the chair next to his to offer Karrie a seat.

"I hate white plastic chairs." Karrie stared disdainfully at the hospital chairs.

"*Hate* is an awfully strong word to use for chairs." Pastor Mike stated as he stood and led Karrie away from the chairs.

"These chairs and I have a history. Something bad always happens when I'm around these chairs."

"Well, you don't have to sit in one if you don't want to." Pastor Mike looked up to see a nurse coming into the room.

"Are you Lo'laini's family?" asked the nurse in blue scrubs.

"I am her pastor, and this is her best friend." Pastor Mike reached out to shake the nurse's hand.

The nurse took off her glove and shook Pastor's Mike hand. "We've just finished her morning routine."

"Is she okay?" Karrie's bottom lip started trembling as she looked up at Pastor Mike.

"I guess it depends on what you mean by *okay*." Pastor Mike put his hand on Karrie's shoulder. "Her nose and her collarbone were broken when her father's truck turned on the freeway. Her knee was shattered, but all those things can heal more easily than the last thing that happened to her."

"What else happened?" asked Karrie

Pastor Mike started to direct Karrie to an elevator.

"Her father died. He wasn't wearing a seat belt, so he was thrown from the car." Pastor Mike stopped and quietly put his hand on Karrie's back while two round tears fell down her cheeks.

Karrie stopped walking and looked at her hands. "So she'll have to go back into foster care . . . She'll hate that. She'll hate that so much, Pastor Mike!"

"That hasn't been decided yet. She might have other options." Pastor Mike held the elevator door and stopped and looked down at Karrie. "Do you want to wait a while before you go in to see her?"

"No, I want to see her."

They entered the elevator and took it to the third floor and walked down the long light-pink hallway, past hospital rooms that each contained two beds. Most of the beds were decorated with bouquets of flowers, with one or two family members clustered around the bed quietly talking and bringing comfort to their loved one. Only occasionally did they pass a lone bed that was not being attended to with flowers or by a loved one, and those lonely beds pierced Karrie's heart.

When they reached Lo'laini's room, Pastor Mike stopped Karrie and said quietly to her, "Karrie, Lo'laini has asked that you not speak to Josh or Tom about this. When people ask something like this of me, I never ask why or try to talk them out of it. I just follow their instructions. Okay, Karrie?"

"Yeah, okay."

When they entered Lo'laini's room, Karrie saw her friend in the bed next to the window. She had a neck brace on, and both of her eyes were bruised and blackened. Her knee was heavily bandaged and then encased in a brace. There was a bouquet of plumeria flowers on the table next to her bed. By the window sat an older woman with long gray-and-black hair pulled back in a simple bun. She had a long dark-blue dress on that hung loosely on her large frame.

"Hi, Karrie." Lo'laini extended her hand to Karrie as they entered the room. "This is my Nana, Aineki Māhoe." Lo'laini pointed to the older woman sitting by the window. Aineki got up from her chair and walked over to Karrie.

"This little girl looks like she needs a hug." Aineki enfolded Karrie into her arms. Her soft arms cooled Karrie's face like Miss Ellen's hug did three years ago. Afterward, Karrie walked over to Lo'laini's bedside and squeezed her hand.

"You heard about my dad?" she asked Karrie, who nodded her head. "Pastor Mike's going to do the funeral. I want people to know my dad tried." Lo'laini looked intently at Pastor Mike. "He really tried, you know. When he got out of jail, he said he had accepted Christ, and he went to church and read his Bible. He went to his AA groups, sometimes every day. It's just that . . . " Lo'laini couldn't finish her sentence as tears fell down her face.

"One night he got weak," Pastor Mike finished her sentence.

"But it doesn't mean he wasn't a Christian," sobbed Lo'laini.

"You're right." Pastor Mike took Lo'laini's other hand. "It doesn't mean he wasn't a Christian. If our weakness could take away our faith, no one would be a Christian."

"But as a proud grandma . . . " Aineki walked over to Lo'laini's bedside and began to stroke her hair. " . . . I would like say that no one tried as much as my Lo'laini."

"Exactly," Karrie squeezed Lo'laini's hand. "So are you going to live with your grandma now?"

"No," Aineki shook her head, "I have a very small apartment on the islands, but Lo'laini has someone else who has wanted Lo'laini to be a part of their lives for many years."

"My aunts are from the UK," Lo'laini said, finishing her grandmother's sentence.

"Well, you always talked like a Brit," Karrie laughed.

"Yeah . . . " Lo'laini looked across the room at a reflection of herself in the mirror. "I look like my mom and talk like my dad. All of my dad's family went to this prep school in Canonbury in North England, and they want to send me there. So I have to move to England, I guess. Karrie, that's why I don't want to see Tom or Josh. I don't want to say good-bye to them. I'm tired of having to say to good-bye to the people I care about."

"They're good guys." Pastor Mike nodded. "And I think they will understand."

"She's got the grades to go to a good school. That will open doors for her I cannot, so why shouldn't she go to that nice school when they can afford to send her?" Aineki smiled at Lo'laini. "Lo'laini's aunts are good people, and they love Lo'laini. They worked hard to make themselves a part of her life. The only problem I can see is, what will Lo'laini eat while she is there?"

"Nana, be nice." Lo'laini laughed.

"I am being nice. It is a known fact that the British cannot cook pork and rice." Aineki wrinkled her nose and continued to say, "They roast pork with no sweet braising, and who would take lovely sticky rice and drench it with cream and sugar to make a wet and watery pudding?"

"It's okay," said Karrie, "Lo'laini will teach them how to cook. Mr. Rodriguez says she's the best cook in the restaurant."

"So you're one of the pastors of the big church near the college?" Aineki looked at Pastor Mike.

"I am the youth pastor." Pastor Mike extended his hand to Aineki.

"I saw your website." Aineki took Pastor Mike's hand and enfolded it into a warm grasp. "It looks like a soda commercial."

"Nana!" rebuked Lo'laini.

"No, your nana's right." Pastor Mike laughed. "We have a committee that puts those things together. I don't have much to do with them."

"Please tell them, Pastor Mike," said Aineki, letting go of Pastor Mike's hand, "that their site is very pretty, but it looks like a soda commercial, and Christianity should not look like a can of soda. Christianity is not a can of soda—it is much more than that."

"I agree," said Pastor Mike. "Christianity is certainly not a can of soda."

"And God is not a refreshing drink that makes us look beautiful and happy all of the time." Aineki smiled.

"No, Nana thinks God is a mother bird." Lo'laini laughed.

"Don't laugh." Aineki frowned at Lo'laini.

"Tell us more about that Aineki," asked Pastor Mike.

"Lo'laini said I thought God was a mother bird because of something I told her I saw this morning. I was walking out of the hotel enjoying the beauty of a gorgeous day, when I was startled by a golden hawk above the tree right outside of the hotel. The yellow and brown wide span of its wings as the bird landed on a tree branch were mesmerizing. I had seen pictures of hawks, but never one up close, and those strong wings were impressive as the great bird fluttered above the tree. I remembered on the news that morning a reporter had said a Golden Hawk had been discovered nesting on top of a building in downtown San Diego. I wondered if this was the same bird, but as I moved toward the tree, I startled the bird and it let out a loud scream, cawing against the wind, and then it was gone. As the bird left, I saw something more amazing. Above the tree a robin was fluttering around, suspended in the sky. Wings outspread, flapping furiously, chest inflated as if the little bird was prepared to do battle with that great hawk. Behind that bird I saw a small nest. I thought how easily the great claws of that hawk could have killed that bird. But the robin stood its ground, prepared to give her life for her chicks even though she would have lost her life in that battle. That's God's love for us," Aineki said as she squeezed Lo'laini's hand.

"Twice in Scripture God compares Himself to mother birds. Once in Deuteronomy 32:11, God compares Himself to a mother eagle protecting her nest, and then again Jesus compares Himself to a mother hen trying to gather her chicks under the protection of His wings in Matthew 23:37," said Pastor Mike.

"But it's not a fair example," said Karrie choking back tears. "I mean God can't die like that robin could have died and left her children unprotected."

"Karrie, remember why we are here," whispered Pastor Mike.

"No, let her speak," said Aineki.

"I'm sorry. I shouldn't have said anything," Karrie wiped away a tear. "God can't die, and God doesn't ever lose. We can lose, and we seem to lose so much."

"You forget Calvary." Aineki smiled. "God lost His Son there, when Jesus, who is God, died."

'But then there was Easter, so He won, there. Where is my Easter with Dad and Mom!" cried Lo'laini.

"Maybe we shouldn't be talking about this now, Lo'laini. All we want you to do is concentrate on getting better." Aineki looked worryingly at Lo'laini.

"But there is comfort in that question," said Pastor Mike. "Your parents' Easter was in their redemption, and now they are in a better place. And one day, you will get to see them again,"

"But what about today! What about now!" cried Lo'laini. "Okay, they are with Jesus, I get that, I believe that, but I still can't see them, I can't touch them, I can't say that I am sorry."

"What are you sorry about?" asked Lo'laini's grandma.

"I'm sorry I got in the truck. I am sorry I didn't stop Dad from driving." Lo'laini sobbed. "I know I shouldn't have gotten in Dad's truck. I just wanted to prove to everyone that he was okay.. I mean, I know he was drunk, but he had other sides to him, too. He was kind and tried to be a good father. I just wanted to prove to everyone who was watching him that night that he was just as good as they were. I wanted to prove he wasn't different than any other Christian in that church!"

"When it comes to life struggles, he wasn't different than any other person in that church. We all have our struggles, Lo'laini," said Pastor Mike.

"I was trying to save him that day in the eyes of everyone at church," said Lo'laini, "and all I did was destroy him."

"He destroyed himself, and that destruction began long before you were born," Aineki said.

Lo'laini wiped away a tear and looked out the window. "Now I feel I am all alone."

"Not completely alone." Aineki stroked Lo'laini's brow.

"No not completely alone." Karrie squeezed Karrie's hand again.

Aineki leaned over and whispered to Lo'laini, "Your parents' redemption and forgiveness ultimately rests with Christ, but there is another part of their redemption that lives inside of you, Little One."

"What do you mean, Grandma?" Lo'laini rested her head on her grandmother's shoulder.

"Their life story will continue to be lived out in your life as their talents, their dreams, their life lessons and yes, even their mistakes echo in your life. Rejoice in their talents and dreams and let Christ help you to overcome their mistakes and you will find there is redemption in the inheritance you have received, Little One, along with pain and beauty."

Lo'laini looked up at her grandmother and Aineki kissed her on the forehead.

"Karrie," Lo'laini whispered, "this Sunday I think you should tell the truth in your testimony. I was wrong about not telling anybody. So I guess I'm saying my Nana's right. When you give your testimony, don't make Christianity look like a soda commercial."

Karrie nodded, and there was a long moment of silence. Then Pastor Mike looked at his watch. "I have some more visits to do today. Lo'laini, do you mind if I pray with you and your family?"

"My family?" Then Lo'laini's face broke out into a large grin. "You mean Karrie and Nana."

"Yes," Pastor Mike said as he took Karrie's and Aineki's hands. "Karrie and Nana are your family."

Aineki slipped her fingers into Lo'laini's hand, and Karrie held on to the other hand. Lo'laini nodded, and Pastor Mike began the prayer.

"Our dear wounded but resurrected Lord, You who were wounded for our transgressions, be with Lo'laini as her wounds heal, and tend to the wounds that will take longer to heal . . . " Pastor Mike's words tapered off in Karrie's mind after he'd said "our dear wounded but risen Lord." That phrase took her back to the Sunday school classroom three years earlier when Miss Dawn had taken a thorn out of her palms and they'd talked about Christ's wounds.

Chapter 23

The following Sunday, Karrie stood in front of the sanctuary microphone again—only this time, the sanctuary wasn't empty. It was full of families and church members who were looking intently at Karrie as she began to speak.

"My name is Karrie, and I've been going to this church for about three years." She scanned the sanctuary over the empathetic eyes who were watching her. Her mother was sitting in the front row on the left-hand side. Josh was sitting in the fourth row, very close to his father; but she couldn't see Tom. "The first time I came to this church, it was with my friend Lo'laini," Karrie continued. "We were both in foster care then."

In the back of the room, Karrie saw Tom and his parents saunter in and take a seat in the back pew next to Alejandro and Isabella. "I've noticed in this church, when someone shares their testimony, they usually share about how things were bad, and that, when they accepted Christ, everything changed, and things got better. My testimony is a little different. I accepted Jesus when I was very young. So young it is hard to remember a time when I didn't know and love Jesus. But things were bad at home, and I got hurt a lot. I got hurt so bad the police had to come to take me away. But I always had Jesus in my life, and that was good."

Karrie voice started shaking, and she stepped back and took a deep breath to steady herself. She remembered what Pastor Mike had said, and she looked at the back wall and saw Pastor Mike smiling at her. It calmed her, so she decided for the rest of her talk she would look at him and no one else.

"Lo'laini loves this church, and she invited me to youth group, and I've come to love it, too. We were both living in foster care when we first came, and Lo'laini and I always felt we had to work hard to fit in. I think we *did* fit in, but we never felt it. Sometimes we would take two hours getting ready because we wanted to look as nice as everyone else. But even still, when we'd arrive at church and see all the people getting out of their nice cars in the parking lot, all dressed so nicely, we felt as though we stuck out like sore thumbs. Pastor Mike says everyone feels that way sometimes because everyone suffers and feels insecure. I think it's true because all of us have been hurt at one time in our lives. I guess some of us just show it more than others. Lo'laini and I used to have this fight about whether you should tell people about what happened to you, because if you told people, they could use it against you. I always said we should talk about it because I want people to know normal people go through these things and that Jesus can help you through this kind of stuff."

Karrie looked up and saw Mrs. Wilson standing uncomfortably in the back of sanctuary.

"I guess you heard my friend Lo'laini is in the hospital. Last night while I was visiting,, Lo'laini finally agreed with me we should always tell the truth about what has happened to us. Some of you saw what happened Wednesday night. If you didn't, Lo'laini's dad came to pick her up, and he was drunk. He was so drunk they got into an accident after they left the church, and now Lo'laini's in the hospital. Some of you who saw what happened may have thought Lo'laini wasn't very smart to get into the truck with her father. But Lo'laini isn't stupid. Lo'laini got into that truck because she wanted her dad to look like a good dad. She wanted what some of you already have—a real family. Pastor told me all kinds of people suffer because of addiction. So you might know what it's like to love someone and want to change them and then realize you can't change them. Lo'laini wanted her dad to be a good dad, and sometimes her dad *was* a good dad. But sometimes he was wasn't. Now I guess she is learning she couldn't have made him into a good dad by believing it to be so. None of us can change the bad things that happen to the people we love, and that is the hardest lesson in the world. But God can redeem them, and that's why I am here talking to you.

"One day, at the restaurant I work at, I heard a pastor say the greatest lesson someone who has been abused can learn is the lesson of forgiveness. But I don't think that's always true. I think the greatest lesson someone who has been abused can learn is how to define forgiveness and learn that abuse isn't normal. 'It's not right, it's not righteous,' as Pastor Mike would say. Abuse is not God's will for anyone, and forgiveness doesn't mean you have to protect the abuser. You don't have to make them look good; you don't have to get in the truck, just because everyone is looking. I think sometimes people make the mistake of thinking forgiveness is making something bad look good. That's what I did. That's not forgiveness. That's just a lie. I like that Jesus never covered the bad but showed everyone what bad really was by being on the cross."

Karrie backed away from the microphone to cough and then looked up and saw Isabella's face beaming up at her from the back pew.

"When I was a kid in Sunday school, I used to wonder why Jesus had scars after He rose from the dead. I mean, if God could make Jesus alive again, why didn't He take away Jesus's scars as well? One day a Sunday school teacher explained it to me. She told me Thomas needed to see Jesus's scars not only so he knew that Jesus rose again, but also so he would know that Jesus suffered, too. I guess we are all like Thomas in some ways. We need to know we are not alone in suffering in this world. I like that we serve a God Who still has scars. So like Miss Dawn told me, three years ago and Pastor Mike told me yesterday, everyone has scars because this world isn't perfect, and it won't be perfect until Jesus comes again. But that's okay, because we serve a God with scars, and His name is Jesus."

Karrie started to walk away from the microphone. Then she stopped and ran back. "Oh, I forgot. I was supposed to share a Scripture." She fumbled through her Bible and found Isaiah 53:5, and then read, "'But he was pierced for our transgressions, he was crushed for our iniquities; the punishment that brought us peace was on him, and by his wounds we are healed,'"

Pastor Mike came up behind Karrie and placed his hand firmly on her shoulders. "Will you join me in praying for Karrie and her family?"

Before Karrie bowed her head, she saw Isabella in the back of the church. She had raised one hand toward heaven as she prayed. Karrie had never seen Isabella pray before and had no idea Isabella prayed the same way Karrie did.

Isabella's brown, muscular, graceful long arm and hand were bathed in red, blue, and yellow lights from the church's stained glass window. Karrie thought Isabella's hand was beautiful.

And they overcame the evil one because of the blood of the Lamb, and because
of the word of their testimony.

—Revelation 12:11f

Important Numbers for Those Who Suffer from Child Abuse or Addiction

ADULT CHILDREN OF ALCOHOLICS
ACA WSO
PO Box 811
Lakewood CA 90714
310-534-1815
www.adultchildren.org/meeting-search

ADULT SURVIVORS OF CHILD ABUSE
The Morris Center
PO Box 281535
San Francisco, 94128
info@ascasupport.org
www.ascasupport.org

CHILD ABUSE HOTLINE
1.800.422.4453
National Domestic Violence Hotline
1-800-799-SAFE(7233) or TTY 1-800-787-3224 or (206) 518-9361

AL-ANON

Meeting Information: 1-888-4AL-ANON (1-888-425-2666)
Al-Anon Family Group Headquarters, Inc
1600 Corporate Landing Parkway
Virginia Beach, VA 23454-5617
www.al-anon.org

ALCOHOLICS ANONYMOUS

A.A. World Services, Inc.
475 Riverside Drive at West 120th St. - 11th Floor
New York, NY 10115
(212) 870-3400
www.aa.org

NARCOTICS ANONYMOUS

1-800-407-7195
www.narcotics.com

For more information about

Rev. Cheryl Anne Kincaid
and
Karrie's Thorn: A Novel
please visit:

www.revcherylkincaid.com

For more information about
AMBASSADOR INTERNATIONAL
please visit:

www.ambassador-international.com

Thank you for reading this book. Please consider leaving us a review on your social media, favorite retailer's website, Goodreads or Bookbub, or our website.

More from Ambassador International

He thinks she's shallow, she thinks he's a nerd. What happens when they are forced to work together?

Team Set Free, a group of young, passionate Christian athletes, strives to lead teens to Christ and help them overcome life's obstacles through practicing Parkour.

The story of an Irish immigrant's quest to save his family, woven together with his present day descendant's story as she works her way to earning money to attend a prestigious art school.